CLIFFHOUSE BY THE SEA

SUNRISE ISLAND SERIES
BOOK ONE

MAREN HILL

Copyright © 2024 by Maren Hill

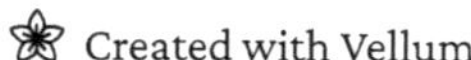 Created with Vellum

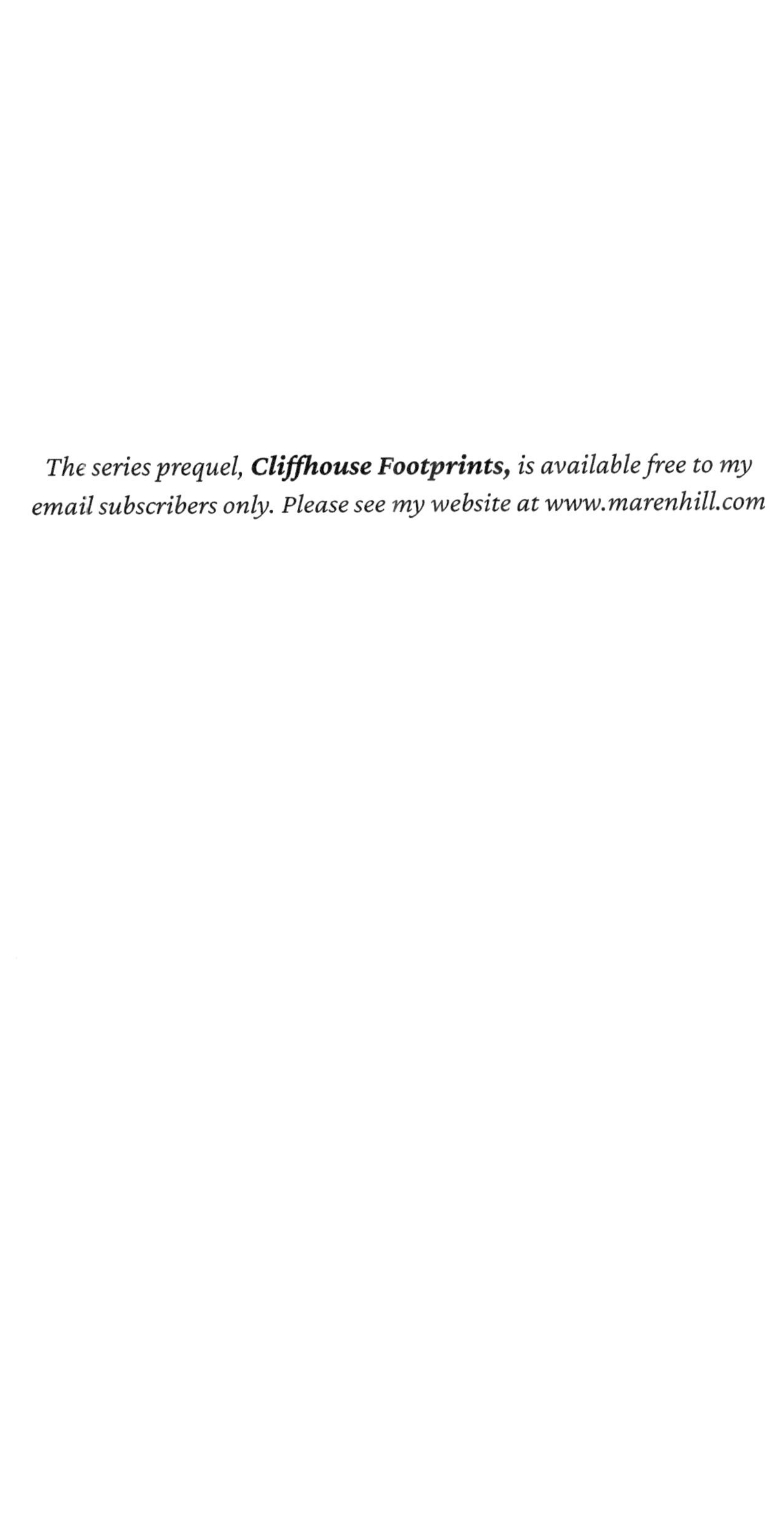

*The series prequel, **Cliffhouse Footprints,** is available free to my email subscribers only. Please see my website at www.marenhill.com*

TRIGGER WARNING

Readers who may be sensitive to themes of losing a spouse and working through grief are advised to proceed with caution.

PROLOGUE

"Together, we can do anything, Jen," Derrick assured. Their love, pure and beautiful, flourished over 20 years on their Sunrise Island farm, inherited from Jennie's mother Kathleen.

Having raised their three children amidst the storied landscape, every corner of the 1000-acre property echoed with tales of generations past. Sharing the responsibilities of farm life, Jennie and Derrick's love story unfolded with each passing season, deepening their connection to the land and to each other. As the value of their property soared, Jennie remained resolute in her commitment to safeguard their legacy, recognizing its irreplaceable significance in their lives.

Struggling to extract the stubborn tap root of a dandelion, Jennie's thoughts drifted to memories of their children gleefully scattering dandelion seeds. Over the drone of a passing helicopter, she called out to Derrick.

"Remember how our kids used to love scattering dandelion seeds by blowing on the flower heads?"

Derrick chuckled. "We did the same when we were kids.

And let's be honest, Jen, we still love blowing the seeds, don't we?"

"Yes, and if you can blow all the seeds off with one breath, then the person you love will love you back," Jennie teased, catching Derrick's smile.

"That's one of the many reasons I fell for you, sweetheart," Derrick replied.

"What? Because I hate pulling dandelion weeds?" Jennie paused, looking up at Derrick, who continued spreading topsoil as they chatted.

"No, sweetheart, because you hold on to the good times. And because, without you, we wouldn't have had our beautiful family," he said, meeting her gaze.

"I can't imagine my life without you, honey." Jennie's voice trembled with emotion.

Overcome with gratitude, Jennie reached for Derrick, pulling him close and sharing a tender kiss. She knew how blessed she was to be living such an idyllic life, with the promise of even more wonderful things up ahead.

CHAPTER 1

Jennie could barely remember the conversation when the police officer called her at home that same afternoon. She had parked her car in the driveway, knowing that Derrick wouldn't need it clear since he was still in Vancouver. With graceful ease, she stepped out of her white Audi, wearing her yoga attire, and glided toward the kitchen entrance of the house.

After cheerfully waving to her mother Kathleen, who was about to exit the greenhouse, and playfully engaging with Rollo's exuberant tail-wagging hello, Jennie entered the kitchen just as the phone rang.

"Hello, may I speak to Jennie Mitchell, please?"

Hearing the somber tone of the male caller's voice, Jennie stopped breathing, as if that might help her listen more carefully. As he identified himself as someone from the Vancouver PD, a chill swept down Jennie's spine. She stood still as a statue, the weight of the unknown settling heavily around her.

The only words she could later recall were, "I regret to

inform you that your husband Derrick died this afternoon in a head-on collision on the Lougheed Highway."

His words hung in the air, intangible, while Jennie tried to grasp their full meaning. She found herself without words, unsure of how to respond. Like other times when something struck unexpectedly, she maintained silence, gathering her thoughts. Searching for any sign that what she heard was a dreadful mistake, she said breathlessly, "It can't be. He'll be home by six thirty if the ferry's running on time. There must be some mistake."

When the call ended, time seemed to stand still as the weight of the news permeated Jennie's soul.

As Kathleen pushed open the kitchen door with a bright smile and a gigantic pink flower head from their rhododendron bush, her smile quickly faded. She found Jennie curled up in the fetal position on the floor sobbing heavily and intermittently crying, "No, no, no."

"Oh, sweetheart," Kathleen exclaimed, "what's happened?" She knelt on the floor close to her daughter and asked, "Is it Derrick? One of the kids? Please, tell me; what's wrong?"

Jennie attempted to stifle her tears, awkwardly transitioning from side-lying to standing. She wiped her face with her hands, then enveloped her mother in a tight embrace, wrapping both arms around her. With as much gentleness as she could muster, she conveyed the devastating news that Derrick was gone. As the words escaped her lips, a quiet acceptance seeped in. At age 39, she found herself a widow. The daunting task of informing her three grown children, Alexa, Kyla, and Nick, loomed ahead.

～

KATHLEEN BREWED A POT OF TEA, and she and Jennie sat in the breakfast room absent-mindedly picking at the leftovers from the night before. An unusual stillness engulfed the house, occasionally disrupted by their hushed conversation.

Their three-year-old German Pointer, Rollo, padded over to Jennie and settled on the floor beside her chair. Glancing at her grief-stricken reflection in the buffet mirror, Jennie recognized a loss that would forever alter the course of her life.

After hugging each other goodnight, Jennie and Kathleen sorrowfully departed to their separate bedrooms. Thankfully, Kathleen had moved to the main floor when she had difficulty climbing stairs.

Alone in her room upstairs, Jennie sat in her upholstered bedroom chair, one of a pair that she and Derrick used to sit in, chatting before bed. Only last weekend, they talked about possibilities for a winter vacation. Jennie had considered Derrick to be an ideal travel companion, particularly because he fully embraced the chance to escape from the darker side of his job as a private investigator. On vacation, he was fully immersed, finding fun in unexpected places. Jennie visualized her and Derrick frolicking in the towering surf at their resort in Antigua, just before beach patrol sank a red flag into the powdery white sand.

Jennie's shoulders trembled, echoing the turbulent storm within. Tears cascaded down her cheeks, her body convulsing with each released sob. The sound of her anguish, a mixture of stifled gasps and raw, unfiltered cries, punctuated the air, leaving her body exhausted.

Her burden temporarily relieved, she mindlessly got ready for bed and faced the night without her beloved husband of 20 years.

CHAPTER 2

Jennie and her 18-year-old twins Alexa and Kyla began making plans for Derrick's service. Her son Nick, age 21, was in his fourth year of the BSc program at UBC. They left him out of the preparations, knowing he could barely cope. To learn of the sudden death of his father while studying for mid-term exams was unimaginable to the rest of the family. They suggested he ask to have them deferred to a later time, given the tragic circumstances.

They would ask Kathleen to gather flowers from their garden to set around the living room where people would gather after the funeral. With a career spent as Head Gardener at Butchart Gardens in Victoria before retiring, Kathleen was a natural choice for the task.

Jennie made tea for Kathleen and her girls. Anticipating their visit, she had set out home-baked cookies to thaw the night before. She arranged them on a serving plate and headed toward the veranda where they had settled. The veranda was always the preferred choice for visits, happy and sad, rain or shine. There was just something about gathering in the open air, sheltered from the elements.

"Oh, no," shrieked Jennie as the plate of cookies met the floor with a resounding crash. Having tripped on an upturned corner of the outdoor mat, she steadied herself to avoid falling. The once neatly arranged treats scattered in all directions, creating a chaotic display of broken fragments. Covering her face with both hands, Jennie attempted to regain composure, but a wave of weakness swept over her. The girls rushed to Jennie's side.

"Mom, are you okay?" they shouted in unison.

"I'm fine, please don't worry, but I'm so sorry about the cookies," Jennie tried to reassure them.

Kyla wrapped her right arm around Jennie and directed her to the nearest soft seat. Alexa cleaned up the mess and, when she finished, she turned to Jennie and said, "Look, Mom, you're doing great, but I'm concerned about you." She stooped down and planted a kiss on Jennie's forehead. Jennie smiled gently, somewhat embarrassed about the tripping incident.

"I have a suggestion, Mom, and I hope you'll take it seriously." Kyla paused briefly before continuing. "Now that the details of the service are complete, perhaps you could take a break and spend a day doing something you love."

Jennie did not resist Kyla's idea. Instinctively, she knew she had to prepare herself to navigate through the most significant personal trauma of her life. When Derrick died, Jennie's world collapsed. Grief left her unmotivated to go anywhere or engage in activities that once brought her joy, like throwing clay on her pottery wheel. When friends called, their voices sounded like echoes down a long, cold metal tunnel. Their well-intended support seemed unattainable, and her world narrowed to the profound loss her family suffered.

Consumed by grief, Jennie felt an ache in her stomach from crying so often. She tried to put on a brave face for her family but, as soon as she was alone, she felt like she was drowning, her body succumbing to the overwhelming tide of emotions.

CHAPTER 3

$\mathcal{J}$ennie took the ferry the next morning to Swartz Bay on Vancouver Island, intending to distract herself by shopping for a pair of gloves. The barn cat had peed on hers when she left them lying around the stables. Experience had taught Jennie that the distinct, ammonia-like odor posed a cleaning challenge. Not up to the task, she would replace the gloves with a new pair.

It was a quiet Monday in the city, with school kids not out until another four weeks. Jennie found a metered parking space right outside the outdoor clothing store on Johnson Street. Pushing open the heavy front door, she glanced around and headed straight for the accessories section. She spotted a pair of black, down-filled gloves sitting on a clearance table. The label told her they were waterproof, a crucial feature in the rainy climate of the Gulf Islands. After trying them on, she made her way to the cash register. Engaging in everyday activities brought her a sense of normalcy and comfort.

Back in her SUV, Jennie buckled up but couldn't bring herself to return home, at least not just yet. With the sun shining and the weather mild, she drove to Clover Point, planning to go for a walk. Some fresh air and exercise seemed like just what she needed.

As Jennie drove past Beacon Hill Park, memories of the joyful moments she and Derrick had shared with their children flooded her mind. She remembered feeding the ducks, petting the spring lambs in the zoo, and watching the great blue herons gracefully glide across the sky like miniature airplanes on their way to feed their young high atop the fir trees.

Jennie found a parking spot on Dallas Road close to the beach she had walked a thousand times. The familiar surroundings provided comfort, yet today, there was a noticeable difference. Without Derrick, she pictured herself as a bird with one wing. It'd never fly again.

Deep inside, Jennie knew she would eventually emerge from the smothering grief that enveloped her. After all, she had responsibilities she could not ignore. But, right now, she couldn't escape the paralyzing truth: She had always shared those responsibilities with the love of her life.

The Victoria area had changed since she last lived there, including the area around Clover Point. No longer the natural landscape she fondly remembered, it now featured concrete walkways and lanes bustling with cyclists of all kinds, skateboarders, scooters, caregivers pushing strollers—practically anything imaginable. Designated areas allowed for dogs off-leash and on. She admired the native artwork in black and red depicting a seahorse painted on the white surface of a rounded structure that, Jennie presumed, had something to do with the sewage outfall located there. City workers attempted to create a natural look with strategically placed rock boulders.

Walking along the sidewalk, Jennie put on her sunglasses and gazed across the water. The gentle southwest breeze brought a welcoming rush of fresh sea air into her lungs and swept her honey-coloured hair away from her face. She inhaled deeply. *In through your nose, out through your mouth*—an age-old mantra from her early yoga days that always resurfaced when she needed to centre herself and relax. Jennie had strong ties to the Victoria area, especially along Dallas Road, where she had spent most of her childhood.

Navigating her way to the lower walkway, she chose the route closest to the water. She made her way out to the wet rocks and leisurely explored the crevices, hoping to glimpse an eel or perhaps a jellyfish. The rhythmic waves provided a soothing soundtrack, and she wondered if she would spot a great blue heron waiting patiently for its next meal.

Jennie eventually arrived at the old boathouse, realizing she would have to crab-walk across the lower concrete wall to reach the boat ramp and continue along the walkway closest to the ocean. She checked to ensure the tide was out, avoiding the risk of getting her feet wet.

Crouching, she patiently waited for the water to recede. She anchored her right foot against the craggy wall wherever she could gain a foothold. Swinging her other leg toward the boathouse ramp, she executed the familiar maneuver she had performed countless times before—sometimes not so lucky with staying dry. She walked across the ramp, stepping between the wooden slats, and continued along the seawall until she reached the rock outcroppings. There, she planned to perch and lose herself in the beauty of nature.

It was Jennie's favourite kind of day. There was a warm, gentle breeze and few people around. She hoisted herself on top of a rock, comfortable in her long coat, and enjoyed the warmth of the sun on her face. With high cheekbones inherited from her mother, and olive skin, Jennie was a natural beauty.

The sparkling glitter on the water's surface captivated

Jennie as she gazed southwest. She had seen it a million times, and it never failed to draw her in—a riot of dancing stars perfectly choreographed to delight and capture the imagination, a result of the sun's reflection on the water. Jennie found herself inexplicably pulled toward the glittering spectacle on the water's surface, as if under some enchanting spell.

As the stars dazzled in the foreground, a swath of shimmering waves rippled in the background like a vast carpet of backup dancers supporting the stars of the show.

Jennie sat on her rocky perch for half an hour or more, as if she were watching the greatest show on earth. Even though it was there for others to see, she felt like the sole spectator. She couldn't deny the notion that, somehow, in the glimmering waves and the dancing stars, was Derrick's soul. *Is he trying to convey a message to me?* She knew it seemed crazy, but she refused to deny anything less than what she genuinely felt at that moment.

A sense of peacefulness and joy enveloped her. *Is this a message from the spiritual world to say that Derrick is at peace? That he will forever be a part of this other-worldly wonder?* She knew one thing for sure. She would, from that moment on, think of her dearly beloved whenever she witnessed the sparkle of sunshine on the sea.

A sudden movement on her right interrupted Jennie's thoughts.

"You look like The Little Mermaid of Copenhagen, the woman ventured, close enough to speak in her normal voice. A moss-coloured T-shirt complemented her off-white Tilley hat. In each hand, she carried a reusable drink bottle.

"I am," Jennie quipped, going along with the story, whatever it was. "But actually, what made you say that?" she asked, not having heard of The Little Mermaid of Copenhagen.

The woman's expression brightened as she launched into

the tale. "The mermaid fell in love with a prince who lives on land. She longs to be with him here on earth and to have an eternal soul like we do."

"Oh," mused Jennie, "wouldn't it be fascinating if we could go back and forth between two worlds?" She tried to visualize Derrick in the spiritual world, but the image remained elusive.

"I'm not so sure I'd like that," the woman said, laughing.

"No, maybe not," agreed Jennie, "but it's fun to fantasize, I suppose. Well, enjoy your walk. It's a lovely day." She looked up, raising her palms toward the sky.

"Nice to meet you," the woman smiled, continuing on her way as Jennie replied after her, "Nice to meet you, too. Thank you." She wasn't sure what she was thanking her for. It was an unexpected interaction that brought Jennie back to life on Earth.

Jennie thought she had better check the ferry schedule on her phone. As she did so, a tall man wearing baggy blue jeans and a zippered fleece passed in front of her, making his way carefully over the rocks below. The white stem of a wireless headphone extended from his right ear, and he carried a paper takeout cup with a plastic lid in his right hand. He stopped a short distance from Jennie, looked out toward two freighters anchored in the strait, and then removed the plastic lid, tossing it among the rocks.

Ugh. Not a local. Well, maybe a local, I don't know. But still.

Normally, Jennie might interact with the stranger, but this was not the day. Instead, she glanced around at the sky. Huge, billowy white clouds surrounded her. She allowed herself time to study the clouds, a pastime she had enjoyed forever. Soon, the image of a person's face tilted upward toward the heavens, arms stretched wide, appeared among the clouds. Next, Jennie imagined the shape of a long-nosed creature with short legs, a fish with two dorsal fins, and then an angel.

She watched as the shapes slowly reconfigured, blending into the vast accumulation of soft cotton puffiness that continued to captivate her.

On the way back to her SUV, Jennie felt her muscles relax, a welcome relief from the exceptional stress of the last few days. She breathed easily and fully, grateful that Kyla had suggested she take some time to herself before Derrick's funeral. The sparkle of the stars would help see her through, going forward as a single parent with a family legacy to protect. If there was a spiritual world where her loved one could be held safe, then she would grab onto that possibility for now.

CHAPTER 4

On the morning of Derrick's service, Jennie moved slowly, trying to get dressed while her mind played movies in her head. She pictured her and Derrick together, riding an elevator up from the ground floor when they first met and started dating. Riding up through life's big events, experiencing the joys, the pitfalls, and all the rest that a full life brings over 20 years. Their wedding, their babies. Raising their three kids in an ancient waterfront home that had been in the family for generations. And now, with their adult daughters employed and their adult son nearing graduation, Jennie stepped off the elevator without her beloved Derrick.

But it wasn't like she left him behind; rather, a tragic and unpredictable event tore him away from her. A head-on collision on the mainland. Alcohol-related. The driver of the oncoming truck crossed over into Derrick's lane, killing him instantly. There would be no coming home to the island they both loved, no planned one last goodbye to the family. The continuing story of their lives together had come to an abrupt close.

Even though Jennie was aware practically every resident of Sunrise Island and others from beyond had assembled for the service, she felt as though she was looking at them behind a translucent wall. Still visible, but barely. She was in her own world, standing there on the edge of the rocky cliff where a restless sea sent swells crashing against the rocks with turbulence that matched Jennie's heart.

Outside, where people gathered on the stony floor, a black telescopic umbrella fell from someone's hands and rolled, stopping some distance from the edge of the cliff. Some watched as Mabel leaned forward and picked it up, a minor distraction from the sadness of the assembly. Mabel glanced toward the family, her lips gently curved upward in a sad smile, while her eyes conveyed deep sorrow. She was one of the many people who had known the family throughout their 20 years on Sunrise Island. When Mabel and Richard faced the loss of their stillborn baby boy, Jennie and Derrick provided unwavering comfort. Later, when Mabel gave birth again, Jennie and Derrick joined in celebrating their profound joy.

They wore white. "Like fluffy clouds in the sky on a sunny day," Jennie said. The family of four, no longer five, stood side-by-side on a flattened stone area of the high clifftop a short distance from the house. Kyla and Alexa tied their long hair in ponytails against the wind. Jennie's short strands would just have to blow where they would because, in the haze of grief, she hadn't given a thought to her hair. And when she glanced in the mirror before heading out to the service, the image that stared back was someone she barely knew.

They had chosen a flattened rock surface on the ocean side of their property, a favourite viewing spot for the whole family, a place where they had watched the ferry come and go, delighted in sailboats with colourful spinnakers gliding along the strait, a place where they had lit fires at dusk and sat out all night laughing, singing, and sometimes drinking wine, maybe homemade cider made by Derrick himself.

Today, standing beside their adult children at the place affectionally named "Grandpa John's Point", Jennie felt satisfied that Derrick would have approved of how they said goodbye. Still, it felt surreal to be standing there today under such sad circumstances.

When the minister stopped speaking, Jennie looked down at the clay urn she held in her hands. Creating the urn on her pottery wheel was the last thing she did for her beloved husband. She had chosen a special glaze containing crystals that held the light.

Together, Jennie, Nick, Alexa, and Kyla left Kathleen's side, walked a few steps closer to the edge of the cliff, and descended the short flight of stairs to a lower landing closer to the water. Jennie lifted the lid and handed it to Nick, placing her hand over the top of the urn to prevent Derrick's ashes from scattering before she was ready. Aware of the smooth glaze of the urn against her hand, she paused for a moment, feeling Derrick's presence. Then, she uncovered the ashes, raised her right arm, and inverted the urn. The wind caught the ashes and swept them away over the Salish Sea. The waters around Sunrise Island would be Derrick's last resting place.

Nick gently reached for the urn, replaced the lid, and held it in his hands for a moment before setting it down. The family embraced each other, together alone, for a few moments before Nick, Alexa, and Kyla ascended the steps to rejoin Kathleen on the clifftop. Jennie said she needed a minute by herself.

Standing alone, Jennie glanced out to sea away from the guests, who stood farther up, waiting to offer their condolences. Jennie was not religious in the traditional sense but now considered herself to be spiritual. In her cherished spot on the family farm with her remaining loved ones close, she felt

Derrick's presence in the ocean breeze, in the water lapping against the rocky cliffs, and in the tall fir trees that graced their heritage property.

Her thoughts echoed back to her visit to Clover Point, where she had experienced a similar moment. Inhaling the sea air, as if assimilating Derrick into the core of her being, Jennie stood in the breeze, gathering strength. When she felt ready, she turned and, with the wind caressing her body, stepped up to join the others.

Some said how fitting it was that the ceremony took place on the property that had been in the family for generations, and how honoured they felt to be in attendance. Jennie graciously absorbed their kind words until a sudden streak of lightning split through the sky, causing everyone to look upward in surprise. Lightning was a rare occurrence on the island, and this seemed to come out of nowhere. A light rain fell, sending the gathering rushing for shelter in the family home.

As abruptly as it had begun, the rain stopped, the sky cleared, and the colourful spectrum of a rainbow arched across the sky. Jennie sensed that this dramatic shift signified an acknowledgment and blessing of the ceremony.

The local Women's Institute had set out an assortment of sandwiches, sweets, and drinks for attendees. Jennie was grateful for their kindness, but she was not at all hungry. She read a few of the hand-written cards. *My heart breaks for you. Prayers to you and your family. We mourn the loss of a wonderful man.* The bouquets set out by Kathleen in the living room joined an abundance of other floral tributes and sympathy cards.

Although genuinely touched by the overwhelming number of flowers, after it was all over, Jennie resolved that she never wanted to see another flower again.

When everyone but her children had gone, Jennie took a deep breath and wrapped her arms around her mother, holding her there in an extended embrace, sharing their depth of sorrow in a silent connection.

AFTER HUGGING HER GRANDCHILDREN GOODNIGHT, Kathleen said quietly to Jennie, "I think I'll turn in early tonight, dear. It's been a long day." She kissed her daughter on the cheek, then slowly made her way to her bedroom on the main floor.

Jennie looked around at her children standing together like ghosts in their white attire and pale, sullen faces. "Now that the wind has died down, why don't we move onto the veranda? I'm sure we could all use some fresh air."

"Would anyone like something to drink?" asked Alexa before heading toward the kitchen.

"Tea, dear, if you don't mind," said Jennie.

"Chamomile, if Mom has it," requested Kyla.

"Hey," said Alexa, "I'm going to make some hot chocolate and melt a huge mound of marshmallows on top, if you have any, Mom."

Jennie tilted her head to her right shoulder and smiled, recognizing that hot chocolate with marshmallows had been the drink of choice for all the kids growing up. "Yes, I guess it's still a standard in this house. I think you'll find some in the pantry, but I can't guarantee the freshness."

Nick had other ideas for his beverage. "If you don't mind, Mom, I'll see if Dad has…," he paused, realizing that he had misspoken. Continuing toward the liquor cabinet in the dining room, Nick began again. "I think I'll pour myself a glass of that Scotch whiskey Dad and I used to share."

Outside, Jennie lit the three tall candles in the hurricane

lamps on the veranda. She found the warm glow of candle flames soothing, and tonight they seemed to offer extra comfort against the darkness.

As Kyla and Alexa settled on the foam cushions of the soft green settee, hot chocolates in hand, Jennie thought about how proud Derrick and she had been of their children throughout the years. He and Jennie had agreed that living on the island probably gave them an appreciation of nature; indeed, each one of them was continually beguiled by a sunset reflected on the water, or a crop of spring flowers growing on the side of the cliff. Nick's dream was to set up a family practice in his hometown. Derrick, especially, had encouraged that and hoped to be his first patient.

The veranda visit was a pleasant way to end the evening after a tough day. Completing the ceremony brought them a sense of relief, and they all seemed satisfied with the way they had honoured Derrick. Nick accepted Alexa's invitation to stay at her place in Grace Square until Sunday, intending to take the ferry back to the mainland. He couldn't afford to be away for long because of the heavy demands of his program.

Jennie closed the door and locked it after her three left the family home. She turned and stared across the living room, which suddenly seemed cavernous despite being filled with tributes. She considered leaving the lights on, even though she and Kathleen were in for the night. Leaving the lights on would not be for reasons of security. They'd only started locking the doors last year when an intruder stole an original work of art from a home in Ganges, just south of the Mitchell farm. But that was extremely unusual. There was barely any crime on the island.

Still, Jennie didn't want to face the night without Derrick. Leaving the light on might somehow deny the darkness, she thought. Then, her inner voice countered: *No, I have to face reality. He's gone. I can't bring him back.*

Reaching for the switch, Jennie turned off the lights, pausing for a moment to adjust to the darkened room. As she moved from the living room and up the long fir staircase toward what used to be their bedroom, the silence was heartbreaking.

She walked into her room and stared at the bed they had shared for 20 years. His side. Her side. The mild indent of each of their bodies was still visible because they hadn't rotated the mattress for so long. Through routine and the busyness of life, sometimes the abnormal becomes normal.

As Jennie slowly prepared for the night, she replayed the attending physician's words in her mind. "He would not have felt any pain." She knew the doctor meant to bring comfort, to assure her that Derrick's passing was merciful. However, as she moved through the motions of everyday life without him, it felt like her pain was only just beginning. The numbness that had shielded her from the full weight of loss gave way, and the reality of Derrick's absence cast a shadow over every mundane task.

Exhausted, she pushed off her shoes and removed her dress and undergarments. From their shared armoire, she selected her velour pajamas as extra warmth against the coolness of the night. She turned the bathtub facets on full, the sound of rushing water filling the room. Sitting on the edge of the tub, her mind replayed scenes of the day. Faces of friends and relatives expressing sympathy and grief the best way they could manage swirled through her head. She had navigated through the seaside ceremony celebrating Derrick's life, but the word *celebration* didn't match Jennie's profound feelings of sorrow.

Warmed after the bath, Jennie put on her pajamas and pulled back the covers. Once in bed, she ran her hand over the surface of Derrick's pillow and inhaled the lingering scent. Positioning her body over the indent Derrick had left behind, she visualized snuggling up to him, just as they had countless times before.

Tears rolled down her cheeks, wetting the pillow. Her soft whimpers escalated into mournful sobs, shaking the mattress like a windstorm coming off the harbour, powerful enough to wake Kathleen.

CHAPTER 5

*O*verdraft. Jennie seldom gave much thought to that term, but now it consumed her thoughts. Ignoring her financial situation had been easy until the hydroelectric bill arrived, forcing her to confront it head-on. Their shared chequing account had always been sufficient for essentials like food, household supplies, and special occasions. It covered the costs of Christmas and birthday gifts for their three grown children, and the substantial expenses, including tuition and room-and-board, required for Nick's education. Garden supplies, animal feed, gas for their two vehicles and the tractor, and regular maintenance for farm equipment were among the visible costs. Jennie was unaware of their expenses for property taxes, insurance, cable, heat, hydro, and water bills, house maintenance, and whatever else was necessary to sustain their vast waterfront property, all covered by Derrick's income as a private investigator and whatever investments he had. But she was learning fast.

As the hydro bill arrived in the mail, Jennie braced herself for extra responsibility. With a heavy sigh, she settled into

Derrick's home office, where his stand-alone computer held the key to their financial records. Thankfully, he had left behind a hidden record of passwords meant for emergencies like this. Leaning close to the screen, she squinted, scrutinizing the online banking statements for the past three months. Her heart sank as she double-checked, hoping the numbers reflected credits, not deductions.

Deep furrows creased Jennie's forehead as she studied the records. An overwhelming wave of frustration and confusion overcame her. *How can I possibly manage the expenses, especially now? Without a steady income? Without Derrick by my side?*

Jennie's gaze fixed on the computer screen but her thoughts drifted away. As the moments passed, a crushing sense of defeat settled deep within her. Like an insurmountable mountain casting a shadow of doubt over her every step, her reluctance to move forward clawed away at her. Despite the overwhelming weight of her emotions, in the deepest part of her soul, she knew she had no choice. She must move on.

Derrick had a knack for numbers, or so Jennie believed, and had seemed to enjoy sequestering himself in the home office tending to business matters. Meticulous in his endeavours, he invested hours in crafting the wood walls of the office, skillfully highlighting the intricate grains of solid oak.

She had trusted him to manage their finances and had assumed he would figure out a backup plan in case he lost his job, either of them became seriously ill, or whatever emergencies might crop up during their lives together. She knew for sure they had insurance because she remembered signing the policy agreement.

Then there were their investments. Jennie had observed Derrick diligently monitoring the expiry dates of their GICs from the sidelines. She had listened to him grumble about the laborious work involved in handling their finances during tax time. *Tax time—was that coming up soon, or was that next March?*

Sighing deeply, Jennie wondered how she would navigate the complexities of gathering the required information, ensuring its accuracy, and meeting the deadlines. Managing the expenses, both apparent and mysterious, on her own posed another daunting question: *Will there be enough money to pay the taxes?*

It was more than she could cope with at the moment. Jennie left the office, poured herself a tall glass of water, and headed for the open veranda. Standing by the rail, she set her glass on a side table and placed her hands on the white rail for support. The crispness of the early morning air provided a welcome contrast to the stuffy office.

She glanced across the property as the sun rose slowly in the east, casting a warm glow over the dew-laden grass. The flute-like, upwardly spiraling song of Swainson's Thrushes drew Jennie's eye to the alder and cedar trees, where a thick tangle of blackberry and ivy provided ideal hiding places for the birds. They were hard to see but easy to hear. Males attempting to attract mates. Maybe warning other birds away from their territory.

Reflecting on her and Derrick's journey through marriage and raising children, her heart warmed with gratitude. But it was still too soon after his sudden demise, and recognizing that a chapter in her life had closed, never to be reopened, she didn't know how she would move forward without her beloved Derrick. Yet, she must, and she knew that she would have to learn how to live the rest of her life without her soul-mate. *My life as a married woman is over.*

After guzzling the entire glass of water at once, Jennie sat in her favourite chair to gather her thoughts. She'd chosen a striking floral pattern featuring pink peonies on a cream background to cover the down-filled cushions and matching foot-stools of the pair, one for her and one for Derrick.

Stretching her legs to reach the footstool, Jennie's thoughts soon returned to finances. She and Derrick had recently discussed saving up for the roof repair needed when water started dripping down the oak bookcase in the living room after heavy rainfall. She envisioned them frantically removing cherished hardcover books out of harm's way, but *Pride and Prejudice* and Moby *Dick* had suffered water damage. Jennie had dabbed the yellowed pages with paper towels, trying to soak up as much water as possible before separating and spreading the pages as best she could, securing the hardbacks with anchors front and back. She set the books over her clothes dryer racks so the air could circulate. "Thank goodness our photo album didn't get wet," she'd said to Derrick, holding the record of their trip to Bermuda on their 10th wedding anniversary close to her chest.

Feeling somewhat ready to continue working on their finances, Jennie returned to the office again, closing the door behind her. Scrolling down to the credit card section, she stopped short when she saw a withdrawal in January for $12,000 next to the name Sunny Daze Travel. *Derrick hadn't talked about a vacation.*

She walked to the kitchen, her heart pounding wildly, her eyes unfocused and darting around the room. Robotically, she poured herself another glass of water. Gulping the entire glassful again, she made her way back to the wrap-around veranda, feeling the blood drain from her head.

Supporting herself with both hands on the rail, she inhaled a deep breath of fresh air. The overdue credit card interest rate had accumulated to $960. *Did he buy a vacation on credit? A vacation we hadn't even discussed?* Jennie shouted these questions aloud, against the roar of a chopper overhead, hoping that her mother Kathleen didn't hear.

Struck with a sudden realization, Jennie felt a rush of tears welling in her eyes. *He booked this as a surprise for our 20th wedding anniversary in October.* Gripping the rail tightly, she sobbed uncontrollably into the surroundings, her stomach heaving in distress.

When the worst of her upset was over, she wiped her face with the sleeves of her cotton shirt, and sat down on the porch swing, shoulders hunched. She felt exhausted, and it was still only morning.

Rollo raced from the lower fields to join Jennie on the veranda. She'd let him out early that morning, and he'd dashed into the distance almost before she could open the kitchen door. His liver-and-white patched head and ticked body increased visibility as he streaked across the fields. Jennie gently grasped his muzzle and looked into his happy brown eyes. She motioned for him to sit beside her on the swing, but Rollo had other plans and soon darted off again, this time toward the barn.

Common sense reasoning told Jennie that, over time, she would learn all she needed to know about her financial state. Fortunately, they'd never hired outside help to clean the house, maintain the gutters, tend the gardens, etc., preferring to do it all themselves. *At least I don't have to fire anyone.*

Jennie and Derrick had shared a sense of pride in continuing the legacy of the family farm. They knew they were luckier than most to own a home. Now it was Jennie's responsibility to figure out a way to hang on to it. She couldn't bear the thought of destroying the legacy because of her inability to manage the finances.

In deep thought, Jennie jumped when a bleary-eyed Kathleen appeared in the front door frame, staring at Jennie sitting on the swing. "I thought I heard some commotion out here. Did you hear anything, dear?"

"Uh, no, Mom, not really. Maybe it was some kids playing in the fields next door, or that noisy helicopter that flew over."

Kathleen took a seat beside Jennie on the swing, pushing her right foot against the floor to begin a gentle rocking. Jennie affectionately touched Kathleen's hand. "How're you doing, Mom?"

Kathleen groggily replied like someone awakened before they were ready. "Oh, gosh," she managed, slowly getting her bearings. "As well as you might expect, I guess, dear. Even though Derrick wasn't my blood, I loved him like my own. We got along so well and…"

Kathleen's eyes glistened with tears and she swallowed hard. "I still can't believe he won't be getting out of his pickup truck, home in time for dinner. And it's been four weeks ago today."

"I know, Mom, I know. I'm just trying to focus on all the glorious memories we made, and trying to put it all in perspective." Jennie knew she was over-simplifying, but she wanted to keep things light and give the impression she had everything under control.

Kathleen chuckled. "Yes, like you do, dear—bring some kind of order to the chaos in our hearts. We all deal with grief in our own way and in our own time. Which reminds me, have you talked to the kids lately?"

"Yes. I try to choose times when I feel strong. Work is a needed distraction for the twins right now, and of course, Nick is busy with the demands of school."

Kathleen nodded understandingly.

Jennie brightened. "I've invited them to stay for dinner on Saturday. They offered to come and help with the chores, so I thought it'd be a good time to have them over." She turned to ask Kathleen, "Is that okay with you, Mom?"

"It'll be great to see them, Jen," she said with a cheerful smile. "I'll make a chocolate cake, Kyla's favourite." Kathleen seemed boosted by having something extra to do. "And how 'bout I make a lamb stew with dumplings for dinner?"

Kathleen still hadn't inquired about Jennie's finances. *Why would she?* Jennie asked herself. *Mom likely assumes everything will tick along as it always has. But she's living in a fantasy world,* Jennie figured. *Maybe that's how she protects her heart. At age 80,* Jennie surmised, *you can only handle so much.*

Jennie was resolute. She wouldn't even hint to Kathleen that things were tight. And she'd do her utmost to act as if everything was okay.

CHAPTER 6

Jennie pondered ways to help pull herself out of the red. Thankfully, there wasn't a mortgage on the home. Her ancestors believed in buying everything outright and, if they couldn't do it that way, they didn't buy it at all. But mounting credit card debt and looming household and property expenses motivated Jennie to find a solution fast.

The chance to visit Alexa and Kyla on Saturday at one o'clock provided a healthy diversion for Jennie. They would meet in Alexa's small apartment on the second floor of the largest commercial building in Grace Square, which was only two stories high.

"Mom, are you okay?" Alexa opened the laminate door to Jennie's quiet knock and embraced her as she entered. It wasn't just the absence of summer sunshine that gave Jennie a worn-out demeanour, and her twins knew it.

Kathleen, too, showed concern. She asked questions such as, "When's the last time you had a medical check-up, dear?

Maybe you should book in with Dr. Shelley before things get busier here on the farm."

Sleepless nights and days spent worrying about how to dig herself out of debt and handle the ongoing expenses took its toll. The dark circles under her eyes betrayed any attempt by Jennie to look like all was well. But she had a plan.

She had asked her daughters to help figure out a way of moving forward. She had let them know of her financial difficulties a week ago, allowing time for the new information to sink in. It apparently hadn't occurred to them to ask. They probably assumed, as Kathleen seemed to, that Derrick had taken care of things. Since Jennie had resolved not to involve her mother, and she wanted to keep the information confidential, sharing the problems with her twins was her only option. She would not involve Nick.

Jennie's first thought had been to ask the girls if they wanted to move in with her. Certainly, she had the room. But she already knew the answer before she asked the question. They were 18 years old and enjoying their independence. Living just steps away from the art gallery where she worked was convenient for Alexa. Having the local dentist as her next-door neighbour was an added perk, especially since he was someone she had been eyeing for quite some time.

Kyla lived in a commune with a lifestyle very different from what she'd have at the farm. So that was out. She and Alexa would continue to pay rent to others, but Jennie assumed her children would want the property to remain in the family forever. Maybe even as a home for their future children.

Jennie and her twins settled in Alexa's cozy living room on handmade furniture Alexa had traded for some of her oil paintings. Taking a deep breath, Jennie began.

"I guess the most obvious strategy would be for me to get a job. But we all know that I haven't worked for over 18 years, and my experience was in human resources management, hardly a sought-after skill here on the island."

The twins nodded in agreement.

"However," Jennie continued, "that's not to say that I couldn't look for work on the mainland, or even in Victoria."

"Mom," said Kyla. "Can you see yourself travelling back and forth on the ferry? That would add hours to your workday. And when the weather's bad," she reminded her mother, "there's always the risk of cancellations." After a momentary pause, she added, "Then, what? You'd have to rent a hotel room."

"And these days," added Alexa, "with all the staff shortages, well, I really wouldn't like to see you adding even more stress to your life."

Jennie sighed. "Oh, I agree, girls. I'm just running down the list of things, so you know what I've been mulling. I'd even thought of working from home—you know, a government job or something."

She rose from her chair and headed to the kitchen to pour herself a glass of water. *This is a meeting I never imagined I'd be having.* She listened to her inner voice for a moment before returning to the meeting. *Keep it in perspective, Jennie. Everyone is healthy, that's what matters. The rest is just logistics.*

Strengthened by the brief interlude, Jennie smiled at the girls, ready to continue their discussion. "I think we all know that selling the farm is just not an option I would consider." The sense of relief she detected from the twins was palpable. "Don't worry, girls. I'd have to be in absolute desperation to think of doing that."

Jennie felt comfort hearing herself say those words out loud to her daughters. These days, she uttered her thoughts out loud a lot, trying to keep things straight in her head. She missed batting around ideas with Derrick, something they used to do routinely until they'd eventually settle on an option.

"I don't know about you two, but honestly, I feel as though Derrick is very much by my side." She noticed the girls' eyes glisten with tears, and her own soon followed. Sadness was as contagious as laughter, it seemed.

"Ahem," Alexa cleared her throat. "Look, have you considered taking in boarders?"

Jennie thought for a moment. "You mean invite strangers into my home? With only me and my 80-year-old mother in the house?" The more Jennie entertained the idea, the more incredulous it seemed.

Alexa's face remained expressionless. "I know, Mom. I'm sure that idea isn't appealing at all. Maybe there's a way to screen people."

Kyla piped up, "You could start by asking for ID, maybe a driver's license, and one other form."

Kyla looked more like Derrick than either of the other two adult children. Today, certain gestures distracted Jennie from her train of thought. The way Kyla raised one brow for emphasis was one of Derrick's traits, but the way she shot her chin in the air to signal the end of the discussion was one of Jennie's traits. Kyla inherited her dark brown eyes and thick black hair from her father.

"Yeah," said Alexa. "And then you could check the validity on Dad's computer. You know, Google the name and see if anything sinister comes up... or if it comes up at all. Maybe do a Canada 411 search and see if their name shows up there."

"What if they're not from Canada?" asked Kyla. Then she offered another suggestion. "I know Dad had ways of finding out all kinds of stuff about people he was investigating. Hey, what about asking one of our RCMP officers to check for you?

They must have special ways of finding accurate information about people."

Jennie chuckled. "All good ideas, girls, but I won't ask for their help. I need to figure this out on my own or not do it at all."

The girls knew that their family, down through the centuries, prided themselves on being self-sufficient. Kyla herself was an example of living that lifestyle.

"What if you looked for long-term renters?" Kyla asked. "Maybe a family with kids. That way, you wouldn't have to be concerned with frequent turnover, I wouldn't think."

"Yes, that's a better idea than boarders, I agree. But you can be stuck with a family you don't, well, like," Jennie said, raising her chin for emphasis. "People can fool you. They portray themselves as all sweetness and light when you meet them and turn into something quite the opposite once you sign the contract. Do you remember when your dad and I used to own that log house on the cliff at Sheringham Point?"

"You mean the one on Vancouver Island, just past Sooke?"

"That's the one." Jennie shook her head, remembering the fiasco. She and Derrick had dropped in one day on their way up island. They hadn't checked up on things since renting it to a couple almost half a year prior. "The renters had allowed their hens to live inside the house alongside them. Chicken poop marred our beautiful river rock fireplace hearth. There were scratches all over the oak floors. Scattered about were pieces of straw, fallen feathers, seed casings, and who knows what?" Jennie shook her head in disgust, remembering the horrific surprise and how foolish they felt for not having checked sooner. But they hadn't wanted to intrude on their tenants' privacy.

"What did you do?" Alexa asked.

"Gave them the boot, cleaned it up, and sold the place."

"Wow. No chicken poop in your house, Mom. Thank goodness," laughed Kyla. "We Mitchells keep ours hens in the coop. They can discard all the feathers and seed casings they want. Everyone's happy that way."

"Okay," said Jennie, enjoying the laugh. "We're making progress. At least we know what we don't want."

They took a quick break, moving to the kitchen to enjoy the freshly baked lemon squares that Kathleen sent along for their gathering. Alexa served dark roast, drip coffee, and a few pieces of her chocolate bar. "Chocolate plus lemon equals bliss," she exclaimed.

"At age 80, I don't think I'll still be making lemon squares," said Jennie. "But I think Mom does it with her eyes shut, honestly."

Kyla took a sip of coffee from her oversized pottery mug, feeling the warmth of the steam on her face. As she set the mug down on the table, her gaze drifted toward the liquor store outside, but her mind seemed elsewhere, lost in thought.

Regaining focus, she returned to the conversation, offering a thoughtful suggestion. "You know, I think your house would be the perfect place for a bed-and-breakfast." Kyla paused, waiting for a response. Since none came, she continued. "The house is big enough and everyone loves a house by the sea."

"Ah, yes," said Alexa, "maybe we could name it Cliffhouse B&B or Cliffhouse by the Sea."

"Okay," said Kyla, "we can talk about names later, but you know, "I like the B&B idea right away for several reasons." Kyla geared up for a convincing argument, hoping to break down the resistance she expected from her mother.

Much to Jennie's relief, the mood was light, and they all seemed to enjoy collaborating on ideas to help save the farm. "Please let us know the reasons, sweetheart," Jennie encouraged, leaning forward with her forearms resting on the table.

"Okay," continued Kyla. "They would be strangers, yes, but you could limit their presence—perhaps one or two nights, or a weekend at most, I'm guessing."

"Yes, that's true, I'd think," replied Jennie. She took some time to ponder how running a bed-and-breakfast could affect her privacy.

"Uh, I'm not sure. I'll have to think about this," Jennie said, her hand absent-mindedly tucking a strand of hair behind her ear. "You know how private I am, girls. I don't want to open my bedroom door and see strangers in the upstairs hallway. And I don't want to share a bathroom with anyone other than family and invited guests."

Kyla piped in, her hands gesturing to the air, "I get it, Mom, but think about the layout of the original house. There are already four bedrooms right there, and the breezeway connecting the original house to the new one allows you to separate your living space from the business."

Alexa added with a hesitant tone, her fingers tapping nervously on the table, "Or maybe you could turn your pottery studio into... no, never mind, a bad idea. You need your joy. You deserve your joy, Mom."

Jennie appreciated the sentiment, but her joy wasn't anything she was thinking about right now. She needed a practical solution to a serious problem, and she needed to put it into effect quickly.

"And guests would need their privacy too," Jennie added, her tone growing more resolute. At that moment, the twins grasped that their mother was seriously considering the idea.

Kyla's eyes lit up with excitement. "We could easily adapt the house for a B&B, Mom. You've got extra bedrooms, extra bathrooms, and a structure that can give you and your guests all the privacy you want."

"We can help you plan it, Mom, if you'll let us," said Alexa, as she rose from her chair and danced into the living room. "I think you've hit on something good, Kyla."

Jennie considered the layout of the house and had to admit that the idea had potential. "You're right. This may be the best idea yet. I'll certainly consider it," she said, smiling at them both. "And thanks so much for offering to help set it up, but I'll probably want to do this myself… if I go ahead with it."

She took a last drink of her coffee and returned her cup to the sink. "This has been a good day," she said. "I needed this. Thank you." She gave each of them an extra-long hug, visualizing Derrick's arms wrapped around all three of them. Jennie's parting words were, "I'll let you know what I decide."

CHAPTER 7

*B*ack at the farm, Jennie studied the hodgepodge structure of their expansive home. The old part, tacked together by her grandfather Robert, consisted of a simple two-story wood frame house connected to a similar structure via the original cookhouse.

That configuration could easily convert to a four-bedroom B&B, leaving my pottery studio private.

The old structure, other than her pottery studio, had been closed off for years, no longer needed once their teens had been out on their own. Jennie strolled across the lawn toward the house attached to the breezeway and pushed open the door.

The air smelled stale. Switching on the lights, she threw back the curtains and slid open the dusty windows, letting in the fresh ocean breeze.

The west-facing unit of the structure had its own kitchen and sitting room and the east-facing unit had a sitting room and dining room but no kitchen. Jennie considered adding the cookhouse kitchen to the western unit. *I could charge more for the bigger space*, she mused aloud, her mind already racing with possibilities.

Hmm she continued, pacing around the room, *I could set up the breakfast room in our dining room. It'd be close to my kitchen, making it easy to prepare and serve breakfast. That way, I could be up and running soon. Maybe in time for some of this year's peak tourist season.*

Jennie's feelings were mixed. She couldn't deny the small well of excitement mixed with a large measure of doubt in her ability to pull this off. Yet, she had to admit that if she were to take advantage of the current tourist season, she would have to get moving.

It's already the end of March, she muttered to herself, a sense of urgency creeping into her thoughts. With a deep breath, she squared her shoulders and resolved to tackle the challenges ahead. There was no time to waste.

CHAPTER 8

*J*ennie couldn't sit still. That drop of dried white paint on the kitchen window above the sink was driving her mad. Reaching under the sink and into the plastic yellow pail where she kept handy cleaning tools, Jennie rummaged through the contents and picked up an old credit card. She walked to the front door, opened it, and walked around the side of the house, standing on her tiptoes to reach the window. Using the edge of the sturdy plastic card, she removed the irritating drop of paint in a few seconds.

Jennie practised the same attention to detail in setting up her B&B. She created lists and checked off tasks as she completed them.

Travelling to Victoria, she bought five sets of dishes, all white and easily replaceable if broken. To decrease travelling time, she purchased extras of everything: cutlery, towels, bed linens, toilet tissue, soap, etc. Jennie had worked feverishly to be ready for the July 1 opening. To allow herself time to focus solely on the business, she enlisted help from the twins with gardening and housecleaning. Kathleen kindly took over meal planning and preparation.

JENNIE CONFIRMED her first booking at Cliffhouse by the Sea for July 1, welcoming a family of four for the long weekend. As the bustling tourist season approached, accommodations on Sunrise Island became scarce, and soon Jennie had fully booked the entire weekend. With demand steadily rising, there was little time for a gradual transition into the business. Cliffhouse by the Sea was up and running, and Jennie along with it.

More than anything, Jennie looked forward to earning some cash.

Returning to the kitchen, Jennie found Kathleen emerging from the basement, carrying a dusty side table. "Mom, your knees. You should have let me carry that," Jennie insisted. However, with a glance at the table, Jennie's perspective changed. "Oh good, Mom; you found it."

Kathleen had reminisced about a table that used to grace the old front hall in the original farmhouse, and Jennie remembered seeing it when she was a child.

"Yes," Kathleen replied weakly, "it's worse for the wear, though." She set the table down on the wood floor and placed her hand on its surface. Applying downward pressure, she rocked the table back and forth, demonstrating its instability.

"Ah, nothing that a good cleaning, a fresh coat of paint, and a few stabilizing nails won't fix," Jennie remarked optimistically. "Or maybe I'll have to glue it. I don't know."

"And I guess you can squeeze that project in between changing the bed linens and the bath towels, emptying the garbage, and cleaning the entire four rooms so they're all available by four o'clock today." Uncharacteristically, Kathleen's tone was laced with sarcasm.

"No, I'll save that project for tomorrow, Mom, when I only have to changeover two rooms. The guests in Number Two and Number Three are staying for two nights, not one."

"I see, " said Kathleen, fidgeting with her apron and glancing away before meeting Jennie's gaze. "Look, I don't see why I couldn't help you prepare the breakfasts." Frowning, Kathleen added, "If everyone comes down at once, you'll have your hands full."

"Not to worry, Mom. I learned organization and expediency from my military father and my horticulturist mother, as you very well know." Jennie wrapped one arm across Kathleen's shoulders and squeezed her close.

Taking a moment to reconsider her mother's offer, Jennie paused, reflecting on recent events. She realized she'd been preoccupied with setting up the business and might have overlooked important indications. Since Derrick's passing, Kathleen has displayed noticeable signs of depression.

A diminished appetite resulted in weight loss she could ill afford. What was once a joyful stroll toward the henhouse, egg basket in hand, now seemed like a chore. When Kathleen returned to the house unsmiling, with a basket brimming with fresh eggs, the change did not escape Jennie's notice.

Kathleen gently freed herself from Jennie's grasp and turned to look at her, her expression full of concern. "Dear, I know you intend to carry on like you and Derrick did. Everything was tickety-boo, and we did everything without outside help. But you are on your own now, dear," she said firmly, her voice tinged with worry, "and that means more work and more responsibilities. I worry that you'll wear yourself out."

Kathleen walked to the sink and retrieved a cleaning cloth from the cupboard below. She cleared a wide swath of dust from the centre of the tabletop, then exposed a clean part of the cloth, and resumed her self-delegated chore.

Jennie felt torn. She was like her mother, always wanting to help, always wanting to contribute. She knew full well that those behaviours brought their own reward. And she didn't want to take that away from Kathleen.

Kathleen gradually squatted to reach for the table legs while holding onto the tabletop to steady herself. As she meticulously wiped the creases, she remarked, "You appear to have a consistently busy schedule."

Jennie glanced at the clock on the stove. "If I stick to my plan, my business will grow," she said confidently, "and I might eventually expand the B&B." She looked at Kathleen, a triumphant smile playing on her lips. "With all this land, the possibilities are endless."

"Ooff," Kathleen groaned as she attempted to get up from her squatting position. She grasped the tabletop, and just as it tipped, Jennie swooped in, placed one hand under Kathleen's right arm, and helped her to her feet.

Smiling awkwardly, Kathleen stammered, "Oh, I should've got up a different way. I can't rely on my knee joints anymore." She wiped her hands on her apron. "I think the floor could use a sweep too," she laughed.

Jennie picked up the cleaning rag and carried the table outside, finding a level spot just outside the door.

Back in the kitchen, she turned to Kathleen with gratitude evident in her eyes. "I'll take that to the barn and work on it later, Mom. Thanks for your help."

With a nod and a warm smile, Kathleen returned to her tasks, a sense of purpose returning to her movements.

In her mind, Jennie reviewed the day's tasks and considered which chores her mother could handle without risking injury or slowing Jennie down when she needed to move fast.

Jennie looked at Kathleen, her eyes full of love for her mother. "You know, Mom, you're right. I could use your help."

Kathleen's expression brightened. "Well, good, Jen. Just let me know. I'll write it all down so I'll remember everything, including what time you want these things done."

Jennie smiled, aware of the sad fact that her mother wouldn't always be around. At her age, each day was a blessing.

"Let's just start with the flowers, Mom. You've always been good at arranging bouquets, and I know you enjoy it."

"Okay." Kathleen smiled. "I don't need to write that down. Let's see, now..."

Before her mother could continue, Jennie interjected. "I'd like you to be in charge of gathering flowers for the breakfast table and arranging them in the vase that's on the table right now. So, it'd be up to you to cut fresh stems, change the water..."

Jennie stopped mid-sentence, a sheepish grin spreading across her face as she realized how ridiculous it was for her to tell her mother, an experienced gardener, how to tend the flowers. "Sorry, Mom, you know the drill," Jennie laughed. "You taught me so very long ago."

Kathleen smiled appreciatively, a twinkle in her eye as she listened to Jennie's plan unfold.

"Now," Jennie continued, "as you know, I always have a fresh bouquet in each room when the guests arrive. Timing will be tricky with guests checking in and out at various times."

"Right," agreed Kathleen, nodding in acknowledgment.

"For example," said Jennie, her voice filled with enthusiasm. "I see that the guests in Rooms One and Four have left, so I'm heading to do the changeovers right now." She paused momentarily, her mind formulating a plan. "Ah, I think I see how this can work, Mom," she smiled. "If the arrangement needs refreshing, I'll simply bring the vase and flowers into the kitchen when I bring the laundry."

"Yes, and if you leave it right here," Kathleen said, designating a clear spot on one end of the counter near the sink, "that'll be my signal to take action."

Kathleen smiled brightly before continuing. "When the bouquet is ready, shall I just take it ahead to the room? How will I know which room it goes to?"

Jennie paused, considering the logistics she hadn't fully mapped."Good thinking, Mom. Tell you what. At the bottom of each vase, I'll use a permanent marker to number each one according to which room it belongs. That way, when you've done your bit, you can replace the vase in the designated room. Make sense?"

"Brilliant," said Kathleen, her eyes lighting up with enthusiasm. "I'll check the counter today in case you bring anything from Rooms One and Four."

"That's one less thing I need to think about, Mom. I appreciate it. And now I must run," Jennie said gratefully. She felt confident that the added responsibility would give Kathleen renewed purpose. She hoped she would again witness the iconic spring in Kathleen's step.

As she headed out the kitchen door, Jennie glanced back at Kathleen, who was preparing to sweep and then scrub the kitchen floor. "Thanks for sweeping, Mom, but as for the scrubbing, please just leave that for me."

CHAPTER 9

"Yes, dear. I admit I'm feeling shaky," Kathleen acknowledged, sinking back on the cushioned settee and tucking a bright pink mohair lap blanket around her hips. Her mother's additional role would have to wait.

After serving tea, Jennie made a suggestion. "Look, Mom, why not stay with Alexa for a while, just for a change of scene? I'm sure she'd love to have you and I know you enjoy poking around the shops in Grace Square."

"What? And leave you alone in the house all by yourself?" Without waiting for a reply, Kathleen emphasized, "Jennie, I wouldn't dream of it."

"Mom, I'm not concerned," Jennie assured her with a confident smile. "People come and go here every day. And I have guests to attend to."

"Jennie, I think we should get another dog," Kathleen suddenly interjected.

Jennie chuckled. "You may be right, Mom. Rollo's more

likely to greet a stranger with his whole back half wagging excitedly than with his teeth barred and him growling."

Alexa said she'd be delighted to have her grandmother visit for as long as she wanted. Kathleen had stayed with Alexa many times and kept her essentials there, ready for the next visit.

Rollo must have heard his name mentioned because he came bounding up to Alexa, his tail wagging furiously. Alexa crouched down, arms open wide, with a grin spreading across her face. "Hey there, Rollo!" she exclaimed, her voice filled with affection. Rollo licked Alexa's face with boundless enthusiasm as she laughed, her fingers delving deeply into his fur.

Rollo was an irresistible, velvety-eared fur baby when he joined their family as a newborn rescue when the twins were 10 years old. As Rollo grew up, they revelled in his spirited companionship, sharing moments of exuberant play and genuine affection. Through the sometimes turbulent, growing-up years, they learned the joys and responsibilities of caring for a pet. Rollo's loyal friendship could provide solace when needed or an energetic frenzy of excitement as they raced around the farm. Alexa said that no matter how glum she felt, Rollo always used his magic to bring her around.

Alexa stowed Kathleen's luggage in the trunk of her apple-red Miata before helping Kathleen into the front passenger seat. Jennie watched as Alexa drove down the driveway, turning right onto the side road.

Shortly after Derrick passed, Jennie looked up the number of Sunny Daze Travel where Derrick had booked the all-inclusive vacation for October. She scoured the fine print, learning about their refund policy. Although the window of opportunity for a refund upon cancellation had closed on June 31 and it was now July 5, she intended to plead for an exception. Surely, there was consideration based on compassion, circumstances beyond your control, or something similar.

Until now, she could not summon the strength to make the call, even though four months had passed since the accident.

Sitting comfortably on the veranda, Jennie held the phone to her ear and heard it ring twice. Jennie was hopeful when she heard an empathetic voice on the other end of the line. To her relief, he agreed to refund Derrick's booking in full, minus a small processing fee.

Jennie smiled to herself. The prospect of having unexpected funds in her bank account was a welcome surprise. With one less concern from the past, things were finally looking up.

CHAPTER 10

"Grandma seems more like herself again, Mom," Alexa reported with relief. "I think all the changes at the farm since Dad died were too much for her to cope with."

"Lexi, I can't thank you enough for stepping in to help with Mom while I focused on the B&B. When she does come home, things will feel a lot more settled. I know how much Mom thrives on routine."

Despite Kathleen's independent nature, Jennie couldn't shake her worries. The thought of Kathleen tripping on the stairs or stumbling over fallen branches scattered by the wind troubled her. She had complained of decreased distance vision in her left eye, and Jennie had meant to schedule an appointment with her optometrist.

As she cleaned the bathroom sink and counter in the unit on the west side, Jennie noticed that the calking needed to be replaced. It had worn away in some spots, and she suspected that the blackened areas were mildew, something she worked hard to keep at bay. In the toughest areas between the bathroom tiles, she'd used a toothbrush dipped in bleach, and that did the job temporarily. She used a glass cleaner around the shower stalls that made the glass sparkle. When her father renovated, he installed marble tiles on the tub surrounds and on the bathroom floors, lending an elegant look to the rooms. Jennie was grateful because the tiles were easy to clean when guests complied with her rule of "No shoes in the room, please." Otherwise, she had to strong-arm stubborn streaks of black shoe marks, one of her least favourite jobs.

So far, her guests seemed friendly and appreciative of what she offered. They often commented on the cleanliness of the room, her homemade breakfasts, fresh floral arrangements, the gorgeous ocean views, and breathtaking sunsets. She had ordered small, round bars of natural soap scented with essential oils and organic herbs so that each guest had a fresh bar for their personal use. Guests often asked if she had any soap for sale.

"No," was her customary reply, "but you can find some of my handmade pottery for sale in that little shop between the accommodation rooms."

The configuration of the original wood-frame farmhouse with cookhouse and the addition of a second house identical in structure lent itself well for conversion to Jennie's bed-and-breakfast business. The eastern side of the structure included the cookhouse that Jennie's great-great-grandmother couldn't do without. The cookhouse had been converted into Jennie's pottery studio before Derrick passed, but had potential for use as part of her business... that was an idea for later should her business take off.

The old cookhouse turned out to be the perfect size for Jennie's pottery studio. Prior to launching the B&B, she had meticulously designed coffee mugs, plates, and bowls, each adorned with her initials and her trademark starfish insignia.

With the B&B up and running, Jennie couldn't find time to pursue her passion for pottery-making and her emerging talent as a watercolour artist. She had little time for many of the activities she used to enjoy. Thankfully, she had enough stock left to offer for sale and she considered asking Bev if she was interested in selling her work in Jennie's shop.

There were four guest rooms altogether. Rooms One and Two included a shared bathroom, living room, and sitting room, while Rooms Two and Three included the same but with the added feature of a small kitchen. Jennie had the option of including the cookhouse, or part of it, as the kitchen for Rooms One and Two. Or, she could install two more bathrooms so that each room would have its own bathroom.

For now, however, Jennie rearranged her pottery studio and cordoned off a small area with shelving to display her pottery and other artwork she might have for sale. She left the front door to the shop open for ease of access by guests and placed a small, handmade sign on the door: *Cliffhouse Giftshop. Please come in.*

It was common practice on the island to offer goods for purchase on the honour system, and Jennie didn't hesitate to do so. Customers would bring their chosen pieces to the breakfast room if it was still open. Otherwise, they'd pay for them at checkout. So far, there hadn't been a problem as far as Jennie could see.

For convenience, Jennie had converted her dining room in the newer house into the breakfast room, closing it at ten each morning. Guests accessed the breakfast room via the veranda, and it was sometimes challenging to usher guests out of there by checkout time.

Today, after changeovers for three of the four guest rooms, Jennie needed to bake some more breakfast muffins and replenish the eggs usually retrieved from the henhouse by

Kathleen. She offered eggs cooked any style, aiming to compete with the best B&Bs on the island. She served homemade bread and preserves, and organic bacon from Stewart Owen's farm, a ten-minute drive away.

The fruit served in a small dish for each guest depended on what was seasonally fresh. Apples from her orchard were plentiful and during the summer months, her fresh strawberries were the talk of the breakfast room. Jennie's fluffy apple pancakes were a hit, and she served pure Canadian maple syrup and creamery butter along with local coffee so good that some drank refill after refill, delaying her breakfast clean-up. Some asked if it was possible to make a reservation for breakfast without booking accommodation. While flattering, it wasn't a consideration.

Wanting a break after completing the routine chores for the day, Jennie took out a frozen pizza to bake for herself for supper. She'd stocked up on frozen pizzas from the grocery store because they were only $3.99, and easy to heat and serve when she was especially busy with the B&B. *It won't be this busy off-season*, she told herself. *I have to make as much money as I can during the summer months. I can relax later.* If there was any fruit left over from breakfast, she'd have it for dessert, knowing it wouldn't stay fresh until the next day.

After supper, Jennie tackled the wobbly end table. It was dusk by then, so she grabbed a flashlight and headed to the barn, closing the kitchen door behind her. Rollo darted out to the forest, leaving Jennie on her own.

She heard the screen door bang shut as she walked down the wood-chip trail to the workshop on the north side of the building immediately next door to the three horse stalls. Grandfather John had wisely located the stalls on the north end, away from the windy cliff on the south side of the old barn. There were large, double doors on both the east and west sides so that farm machinery could be driven in and out from either end.

Because her father had had the foresight to electrify the barn, she could work on the table at night. There was a work-table against the far wall and an overhead light. She lifted the end table onto the workstation, resting it upside down so she could study the construction. Derrick's thoughtful addition of an organized tool wall when they first moved in allowed Jennie the convenience of having everything she needed at a glance. *Still helping me out, my love.*

Jennie examined how the legs attached to the tabletop, noting the absence of screws, signifying that glue held the pieces together. She surmised that, as the glue aged, the pieces gradually loosened—she recalled the sharp cracking sound in one of her antique chairs when her son Nick had shifted his weight one time at dinner.

Determined, Jennie removed one of the three hammers from the wall, planning to drive the nail at an angle from the top of each leg to the underside of the tabletop. Finding some nails in a glass jar, she held the hammer in her right hand, ready to tap the nail into the wood, careful not to use too much force to prevent splitting the wood. It appeared to be a straightforward fix.

After a few taps, Jennie noticed the nail wasn't going in—the wood was too hard. She readjusted her grip between the nail head and stem, swung back the hammer, and striking with greater force, accidentally slammed the hammer against her thumb and forefinger. Recoiling, she headed for the sink, letting the hammer and the nail fall where they might. "Holy man, that hurts!" she shouted out to the rafters. Turning on the tap, she ran cold water over her throbbing thumb and fore-finger to help ease the pain.

Jennie glanced at her phone... 8:13. As a wave of fatigue

washed over her, she stared out the open barn door into the darkness and decided it was time to quit. A sudden movement caught her eye as she searched for her flashlight.

A quick, indrawn breath revealed her horror at seeing the tail end of a rat disappearing into the shadows. Jennie's muscles tensed in unison, leaving her frozen in place as her heart pounded in her chest. Frightened, yet unwilling to let her guests hear her distress, she gritted her teeth and muttered under her breath, "Ugh, I can't stand rats. Please, no, don't let there be rats here."

She grabbed her flashlight, turned it on, flicked the light switch off before leaving the barn, and hurried out the door. In the pitch-black darkness, with the moon and stars hidden by the clouds, she realized she had forgotten to turn on the outdoor lights around the house and yard.

Sweeping the flashlight incessantly back and forth around her feet as she approached the kitchen door, her thoughts consumed by the rat, Jennie forcefully swung open the screen door. She let it rest against her body while she grasped the knob of the inner door, only to find it locked.

She turned the knob right and then left as much as it would allow. "Oh, no, please don't tell me I've locked myself out," she muttered, continuing to jiggle the locked knob back and forth. A sudden panic. Another sweep of her flashlight, first around her feet, then out into the yard toward the barn.

Deciding to attempt entry through the veranda, she shone the light to make a pathway. Crossing the wood floor, she extended her hand toward the doorknob that led to the front hallway, praying she had left that door unlocked.

No such luck.

Jennie zipped up her hoodie and pulled the hood over her head. The cloth covering seemed to offer distance from the rat and provide a sense of comfort. Perching on the settee to gather her thoughts, she continued to sweep the flashlight back and forth across the floor. *Oh my gosh, I sure hope the batteries are okay.*

Jennie had missed dinner and started feeling weak. *No, think*, she commanded herself. *What are my options?* She considered calling her mother to check if she had her key to the house with her, but then Jennie remembered she didn't have her car keys since they were in the locked house. Even if Kathleen had a house key, Jennie couldn't retrieve it, and she didn't want to burden Alexa by asking her to deliver it when she'd be driving Kathleen back to the farm the next day.

I'll have to break in, she decided, fully aware that her father had made the house pretty secure. However, as well as every self-respecting burglar knew, anyone could get in if they put their mind to it. So, she put her mind to the task.

Rising from the settee on the veranda, Jennie walked around to the kitchen window closest to the door and illuminated it with her flashlight. The window was open about an inch. She retraced her steps, remembering to sweep the ground for rats, and carried a solid wood chair down the veranda steps, setting it down below the kitchen window.

Finding two big enough rocks by the edge of the driveway, she strained to carry them closer to the window. Placing the rocks side-by-side, she propped the flashlight between them for support and shone the light strategically on the window so she could see what she was doing.

Standing on the chair, she removed the screen and slid open the top half of the window, the only part that opened. Jennie felt like a victorious cat burglar. But she wasn't in yet, and the window was high up.

Now, to hoist myself up. Hanging onto both sides of the window frame, she put her right foot on the chair back and boosted herself up high enough to push the top half of her body into the opening.

Now what? Awkwardly, she bent her left knee and brought her left foot up onto the window ledge while easing her right leg and her top half further toward the kitchen counter. Her other leg followed, and she was in. Amazed that a human could fit into such a small space, she planned to rethink her home's security.

Pausing for a moment on all fours, she waited until she felt ready for her next move. She turned her body around so she could stretch her left leg until it reached the floor, and then maneuvered the rest of her body until she stood upright. "Alleluia!", she shouted out loud, raising both arms in the air like an Olympic medal-winner.

She stood on a kitchen chair to close and lock the window. Taking a moment to breathe, she remembered the flashlight. Unlocking the main kitchen door, she swung it fully open while leaving the screen door shut against any rodent intruders.

Jennie flicked on the outside lights, opened the screen door, and darted out to retrieve the flashlight still perched between the two rocks.

Returning with the flashlight in hand, she firmly turned the lock on the kitchen door with a sense of closure, as if to leave her troubles behind. *That was quite the night,* she mused, checking the time on her phone: 9:30 p.m. In just 7 ½ hours, her alarm would alert her to get up, shower, and prepare breakfast for the eight guests in the four occupied guest rooms.

Crunching on a bowl of boxed cereal before bed, Jennie headed up the stairs in the quiet house. Then she remembered Rollo. The last time she'd seen him was when the guests in Room 1 headed out the driveway. She had called him away from chasing the car onto the side road, and he had eagerly raced toward her waiting for his reward.

What else could go wrong today?

It was unusual for Rollo not to stay close to the house when the family was there. She threw on her familiar black sweater, which always hung on the coat-hook in the hall, and stepped out onto the veranda.

First, she tried calling Rollo with her normal voice, not wanting to awaken her guests. When he didn't appear, she had no choice but to yell.

"Roollooo," she shouted, elongating the vowels. First, she turned her head to shout toward the east, toward the orchards. Next, toward the north, where the side road intersected with their driveway.

Retrieving another flashlight from the barn, she walked toward the southwest, shouting toward the cliff.

Still nothing.

It was unusual for Rollo to stray. *Maybe there's a dog in heat*, she thought, before remembering her parents had him neutered when they adopted him.

Considering her options and the hour, Jennie concluded she could do no more that night and would look for help in the morning. Just as she was about to open the unlocked front door, she heard a young voice call to her from the vicinity of the kitchen.

"Jennie, are you looking for Rollo?"

Rollo ran toward Jennie, his back half wagging victoriously as if he had been just released from prison. "Okay, okay, Rollo. Settle down. You're home now," Jennie assured him, patting him vigorously on his side. She opened the front door and Rollo darted inside, heading toward the kitchen and his food and water station.

"Where did you find him?" Jennie asked the obvious question.

"Oh, uh," stammered the boy, hands in his pockets and looking toward the ground before looking up at Jennie. "Mom's out for the evening, and Rollo is so friendly that I thought I'd spend some time with him."

"You mean you've had him in your room all this time without asking permission?" Jennie's high-pitched voice caused the boy to shrink back.

"I know. It was stupid of me. I'm sorry."

Jennie sighed. "Did you give him any food or drink?" she asked, hoping he didn't give him anything toxic, like chocolate.

"Yes, I gave him some chips. That's all we had," he said, "but he didn't really like them. So, we just watched TV together and sat around. When I heard you calling for him, I brought him back right away."

Jennie felt utterly exhausted by now. She said goodnight to the boy, fully aware of their impending checkout the next morning. It didn't seem worthwhile to admonish him about taking her dog without permission, especially considering their imminent departure. Once more, Jennie trudged up the stairs to retire for the night.

CHAPTER 11

A wide smile lit up Kathleen's face as Jennie greeted her and Alexa outside the kitchen entrance. Rollo's exuberant welcome nearly bowled Kathleen over before Alexa deftly diverted him, playfully alluring him toward the barn.

"Mom, welcome home," Jennie said, her grin mirroring Kathleen's warmth as she enveloped her in a hug. "You look wonderful. How was your stay?"

"As much as I love staying with Alexa, it's always great to be home," Kathleen replied, her gaze sweeping over the property. "I'm not used to seeing so many cars in the yard, but I guess that's a testament to the success of your B&B, dear," she acknowledged with a smile.

As Kathleen settled back in, Jennie noticed a newfound energy in her demeanor. On her first morning back home, Jennie observed Kathleen deeply engaged in conversation with a couple from Arizona, her enthusiasm evident in her animated gestures and bright smile. As Kathleen resumed her duties of floral arranging and egg gathering, Jennie felt reassured by Kathleen's renewed sense of purpose.

But, as Friday unfolded, a gradual sense of heaviness settled over Jennie. The initial energy that propelled her through the morning and afternoon chores waned, replaced by an encroaching weariness that seeped into the very fabric of her being.

When her cell phone chimed to life at 7:05 that evening, she considered letting the call go. Noticing Bev's name flash across the screen, a warm smile lit up Jennie's face, and she couldn't resist answering.

Jennie first met Bev when she and Derrick had moved to Sunrise Island, and they have been the best of friends ever since. Bev soon introduced Jennie to pottery-making, a skill that Jennie grew to love, and she became good enough to sell her wares at the popular Sunrise Island market on Saturdays. Bev, also known for her oil paintings of local scenes, was inspirational in Jennie's new venture into watercolour painting.

"Bev, I want to chat but, in all honesty, I'm just beat. Do you think we could meet tomorrow morning, say around 11:30, at the Treehouse?"

...

On Saturday they chatted happily on the hard wooden benches at the Treehouse Café, a popular gathering place for locals and visitors alike.

"It's been far too long, Jen. I won't even ask what you've been up to since our last yoga class," Bev chuckled, her laughter infectious.

Jennie returned the smile. "Things change, but not much. I do plan to resume the classes, but not until after the harvest."

As The Treehouse hummed with live music, a small jazz band serenaded the crowd, filling the air with a sense of camaraderie. The familiar strains of "Enjoy yourself, it's later than you think," reached their ears, prompting shared laughter between the two friends.

"Could that be any more appropriate, Jen?" asked Bev.

"I know, I know. It seems to be a common theme among my friends these days. But honestly, I love running the B&B. Yes, it's hard work and I'll admit sometimes I feel like ditching the entire works."

Allowing herself to say those words, Jennie knew that her dearest friend offered a safe haven for her deepest fears. Bev leaned forward slightly, her eyes fixed on Jennie's with unwavering attention, encouraging her to continue.

"If the business thrives or fails, it's all on me." Jennie lowered her voice, confiding in Bev. "The thought of failure is unbearable, to be honest, Bev. I took a leap of faith, forging a pathway without Derrick by my side. If I'm unsuccessful, it'll highlight the fact that I can't make it without him."

A soft, understanding smile graced Bev's lips, radiating warmth and empathy.

"I know you feel the responsibility of carrying on the family legacy. Jen. What you've created is truly amazing and your success speaks for itself."

Jennie nodded, grateful for Bev's perspective. "I guess I just worry that I'm not doing enough."

With a knowing look, Bev gently countered, "Perhaps you're being too hard on yourself. It's okay to ask for help, you know."

Jennie chuckled softly. "I suppose old habits die hard. But you're right, I could ask for help."

"Hey, Mom, nice to see you relaxing for a change." Alexa approached their table unexpectedly. She smiled warmly at both and greeted Bev with a friendly nod. "And Auntie Bev, so nice to see you too."

Bev and her husband divorced years ago before Bev moved to Sunrise. Not having any children of her own, she became close to Jennie's three, especially the twins.

The sun caught Bev's short, red hair, highlighting a shade that looked anything but natural, Jennie thought. But that was Bev. She laughed a lot and didn't fuss with things as menial as hair colour. Shorter than Jennie at 5'2", her rounded figure seemed to suit her relaxed demeanour.

Bev was the same age as Jennie, 39. Despite their differences, Jennie felt comfortable with Bev from their first meeting, as if she'd known her for years. Over time, Jennie learned Bev was friendly to everyone, but a fool to no one.

Alexa perched on the corner of the bench as if she were staying for only a minute.

"Lexi," Jennie exclaimed, "I thought you were going to Vancouver this weekend to say hello to Nick." Her brother was in his final year of the BSc program at UBC.

"Nah, he's studying for exams, I found out, so we'll do something when the stress is off."

"Is he managing any better, do you think?" asked Jennie. Nick had considered dropping out every year since the beginning but advanced to his graduate year, barely.

"Still has anxiety, unfortunately. He's not sleeping well."

Jennie's heart sank. "Oh, that's not good news, Lex. I wonder if I should go over there, maybe take him out to dinner —something for a change of focus."

"Mom, you're so thoughtful but, honestly, I think he has to learn to manage this himself."

"I know, dear, but sometimes people need a bit of help," Jennie said, pausing for a moment to consider how she might help. "He loves Italian food, so maybe I'll take him for a meal at Antonio's."

"Nick keeps telling me this joke about medical school students," Alexa chuckled, shooting a glance at both Bev and her mom, making sure they were listening. "I think it's become his mantra now."

"Oh, you mean the one that goes, 'What do you call the student who graduates with the lowest marks?'" Jennie asked, rolling her eyes.

"Yeah," smiled Alexa, "that one."

"Huh?" asked Bev, looking eager to know the answer.

"Doctor," said Jennie, and they laughed harmoniously. "Well, if that makes him relax, then it's a good mantra."

"Uh, I have some news of sorts," said Alexa, lowering her voice to almost a whisper. "He has a new girlfriend, you know."

Jennie's breathing slowed for a moment, and her features softened, as if a tapestry of thoughts unravelled in her mind.

Emerging from deep thought, Jennie exclaimed, "Oh, that changes everything. He probably doesn't need Mama's help anymore." She tossed her head back, and a cascade of laughter spilled from her throat.

Jennie felt confident she had made the right decision not to interfere. She knew nothing about the new relationship but hoped it gave her son a new, positive energy.

"Have you had lunch, Lexi?" Jennie asked.

"Yes, and I'm going to meet my friend Graham down at the dock. We're going kayaking."

"Perfect day for it, Bev said."

After bidding her mother and Bev to enjoy the rest of their day, Alexa skipped away toward the dock.

"You know," Bev said after Alexa left, "we should do that sometime, Jen. What do you think?"

"Yes, definitely, but not until the market shuts down for

the summer, the harvest is over, and I have some spare time on my hands. Is that okay, Bev?" The Saturday market was a huge draw for tourists and now that Jennie was part of that industry, she wanted to take full advantage.

"So be it, my dear. I'm easy. Just let me know when the time is right."

The server swept in with two dishes balanced on her forearms. She placed the smoked salmon salad in front of Jennie and the bread pudding with poached eggs and salad in front of Bev. "Oh, these look delicious," remarked Bev, picking up her fork as the server refilled their coffee mugs.

Jennie studied the food presentation. "I wish I was better at arranging food on the plate. Not that I even try, I admit."

"I didn't know it was tricky," laughed Bev, lifting a mouthful of salad toward her mouth.

"Oh, you know what I mean. That looks like a work of art. For me, with the day-to-day, I just spoon it onto the plate, not giving a second thought to where it lands—unless it's breakfast for my guests, of course," she added hastily.

After a moment of reflection, Jennie added, "For me, I guess meals are mostly something to get over with before going on to the next work project.

When they finished their brunch, Bev and Jennie browsed in the shops. Carrington's stocked a plethora of goods of every kind. If you needed something, you could usually find it at Carrington's, and if not, they would order it for you so you wouldn't have to take a ferry to shop elsewhere.

CHAPTER 12

Time raced by with Jennie engrossed in the ever-increasing demands of running the B&B as well as the farm. She still found herself with little time to pursue other interests and enjoy her relationships with friends and family.

It was Saturday, March 2, 2019, one year since Derrick's fatal accident. Jennie's memory would likely hold the date forever.

As the alarm rang, Jennie did something she rarely does: she hit the Snooze button. When it rang a second time, she hit it again. On round three, she made herself get up.

After a quick wake-up shower, she descended the stairs to the kitchen and began her daily routine. She set the dining room table for breakfast, checked the floral arrangement for freshness since Kathleen wasn't home, and aligned the chairs. Kathleen wanted a change of scene after a dreary winter season and Alexa eagerly welcomed another visit with her cherished grandmother. Alexa anticipated the delights of Kathleen's home cooking, even if it meant inevitably gaining a few extra pounds.

In the kitchen, Jennie prepared for the breakfast service, setting out cookware and ingredients. She pre-measured flour and sugar for the apple pancakes, measured tablespoons of finely ground coffee into the baskets of the two coffee makers, poured 12 cups of water into each reservoir, and set the timer to 6:45.

As she worked, Jennie realized the need for more energizing music and changed her playlist to *Random Access Memories* by Daft Punk.

Jennie's thoughts drifted back to her rude awakening at 5 a.m. The irony of the term "alarm" struck her—indeed, it was alarming to be jolted awake so early. She chuckled at her witticism as she poured herself a cup from the French press. The coffee seemed to taste better than usual, she noted, as things often do when one apparently is in desperate need.

When all the preparations were done, she boiled herself an egg and toasted a piece of grainy bread. Feeling the need for an extra pick-me-up, she slathered more butter than usual on her warm toast and followed that with a thick layer of their home-made strawberry jam. Jennie held the jam jar close to her nostrils and inhaled the sweet scent reminiscent of last summer's strawberry harvest.

Breakfast extended over the full two hours that morning, with eight guests arriving at various times. Some wanted poached, some fried, and some scrambled. Jennie had the apple pancakes and crispy organic bacon warming in the oven and had set out the juice, muffins, and fruit bowls before any of the guests arrived.

As she exited Room Two with an overflowing laundry basket, she noticed a black SUV making its way up the driveway. The bright yellow flowers of their forsythia bush caught her eye, and Jennie visualized Derrick using a Dutch hoe to keep the weeds at bay. *Keeping things tidy for our guests, love.* A bittersweet smile formed on Jennie's lips.

The SUV rolled to a stop at the turnaround. The driver's door swung open, revealing a tall, lean man wearing denim jeans and a sky blue, short-sleeved T-shirt. As he stepped out, Jennie couldn't help but notice his curly, salt-and-pepper hair, estimating him to be a few years older than herself, maybe 43 or 44. His chiseled face and attractive physique immediately caught her attention, with his broad chest and muscular arms only adding to his allure, she observed. Not that Jennie was actively seeking to be drawn to any man, she reminded herself. Yet, she couldn't shake her awareness of the stranger's appearance. *Some things just can't help themselves*, she mused with a wry chuckle.

He approached her with an effortless stride, his long legs striking in blue jeans.

"Morning," he greeted. "Beauty of a day, isn't it?" His smile lit up his face, and as he got closer to Jennie, she couldn't help but notice his turquoise blue eyes, accentuated by his blue T-shirt.

"Yes, it's just lovely. How can I help you?" Jennie set down the laundry basket to help preserve her energy.

"I'm Clay Brookfield," he said warmly, extending his hand. "You must be Jennie."

Jennie shook his warm, calloused hand, wondering how he knew her name.

"Your mother mentioned that I should chat with you about renting a spot on your clifftop," Clay said, his eyes widening with sincerity, causing Jennie to pause. His easy-going manner provided a welcome contrast to the down-to-business attitude Jennie acquired, now that she had a business to manage.

There was a charismatic charm to Clay that immediately captivated Jennie. *Maybe I should give this... whatever it is... some consideration. Mom wouldn't have sent him my way if she didn't think it could be worthwhile.*

"Haha, well, this is quite unexpected," Jennie chuckled, raising her brows in surprise as she allowed herself a moment to consider his request.

"I see you're busy, Jennie, " Clay said considerately, "and I don't want to take up your time." He held his hand up to shield his eyes from the morning sun.

"If you don't mind," Jennie said, lifting the laundry basket and resting it against her left hip more gracefully than usual, "I just need a minute to start this load of laundry, then I'll be right with you."

Jennie maintained a pleasant smile, despite feeling uneasy when Clay pressed his palms together in a gesture resembling a prayer. He bent forward slightly as if to bow, and with a friendly smile replied, "Yes, of course, I'm in no hurry."

Jennie had encountered the gesture before. She did, after all, live on Sunrise Island, where a significant portion of the population were hippies or naturalists. She wasn't sure what they preferred to be called these days. One thing she knew for sure was that her daughter Kyla did not refer to herself as a hippie, despite living in a commune.

Sweeping her free arm toward the veranda, Jennie said, "Please, have a seat. I won't be long."

"Thanks," he replied. "Please take your time," Clay said, heading toward the veranda.

Jennie noticed Clay had a demeanour that suggested he rarely rushed. He seemed peaceful, a stark contrast to how Jennie felt almost all the time these days.

Jennie proceeded to the kitchen and then to the laundry room, which she and Derrick had added as their kids and their clothes had increased in size.

Having placed the laundry into the top-loading washing

machine, Jennie walked toward the main entrance of the house, opened the heavy oak door, and stepped out onto the veranda. She found Clay near the steps, playing with Rollo.

Turning to look at Jennie, he asked, "What's his name?"

"Oh, that's Rollo," she said, her lips curved upwards on the left side, a family trait passed down from her father's side. "He's a rescue. Nine years old now."

"Lucky dog," Clay remarked, ascending the steps and following Jennie's cue to have a seat. "It looks like a fabulous location here at Cliffhouse by the Sea." Clay fell silent for a moment, running his fingertips over the hills and valleys of the wicker armrest. He bounced his right knee.

"Now," Jennie continued, curious to learn what Clay had in mind. "Please tell me about your idea to rent my clifftop."

Clay leaned forward in his chair. "Well, as I mentioned, I teach paragliding."

"Yes," said Jennie, nodding. "I suppose that explains the graphics on your vehicle," she remarked, studying depictions of paragliders with colourful kites soaring above grassy cliffs, overlooking sparkling water with a mountainous backdrop. Jennie surprised herself by teasing the handsome stranger; it was not her style.

Clay continued. "I'm looking for a place where I could teach paragliding to small groups or even just individuals. And this seems like a good launching spot." He paused, waiting for a reaction, but Jennie remained silent, prompting him to continue.

"My property is inland, so I launch from Bruce Peak, but that's not ideal for teaching students because there's limited access to a landing field."

Jennie was curious. "What about Mount Maxwell?"

Clay shook his head. "No, paragliding in a public park is against the law here on the island. You may have seen them paragliding at Clover Point in Victoria, but that's a different story," he explained. "The open space and higher elevation you have here would be perfect for my purposes," Clay said, gesturing toward the clifftop.

"Ah," said Jennie, "I get it now. And how might I benefit from allowing you to use my land for your purposes?" Jennie was secretly proud of the business acumen she'd built over a short while.

"Oh, I'd pay you, of course, maybe on a month-to-month basis, whatever might suit you."

Jennie wanted Clay to suggest a figure because she had no idea what she might charge for the use of the clifftop. "What kind of money did you have in mind, Clay?" she asked directly.

Clay pressed his lips together before answering. "I was thinking something near $400 a month," he ventured.

I could use the extra money, that's for sure. But I don't know if I want to give up more privacy. Jennie pictured a group of students trooping across her fields hauling their equipment.

"Well, I'd need some time to think about it, Clay," she smiled. "This is quite unexpected, as I've said, and I need to understand exactly what would be involved."

Rising from her chair, Jennie extended her hand. "Thank you for stopping in, Clay. It's nice to meet you."

Clay rose from his chair. "Yes, I'm so sorry for the intrusion," he said apologetically. "Is there some time that we could meet to discuss it further?"

Clay's striking appearance again took Jennie by surprise. That she even noticed another man so soon after Derrick's passing was nothing short of shocking to her. Not that she could see herself entering into another serious relationship. Ever.

Jennie looked toward the orchards but was hard-pressed to

find a time when she might be free. She tilted her head to her left shoulder and laughed softly.

"You know, it's just crazy how busy I get," Jennie said, shrugging her shoulders slightly, "but surely to goodness, I can spare half an hour to listen to your ideas. I have only one changeover tomorrow, so that means less work for me." She paused, lifting her hand to her chin in contemplation.

"After I clean up the breakfast room and prepare for the guests arriving early at two, then yes, I could meet you at six o'clock. That should account for guests arriving later than the 4 p.m. check-in." Her fingers tapped lightly on the table to emphasize the time. "Would that work for you?"

Clay smiled broadly. "Thank you, that'd be great, Jennie."

Please don't do that hippie thank-you thing, Jennie pleaded in her mind.

Clay headed toward the veranda steps, and then stopped, turning toward Jennie. "I wonder if you wouldn't mind me taking a quick walk over there," he said, pointing west toward the clifftop, "so I can have a better idea of the layout? That way, I'll know exactly what to ask of you when we meet tomorrow."

"Be my guest," Jennie replied, proud of herself for being open to a new idea. "I'll see you here tomorrow, at six." She watched Clay as he sauntered toward the clifftop, again noticing his well-toned physique. *Maybe I should take up paragliding.*

CHAPTER 13

Jennie had paced up and down for fifteen minutes and was about to give up on Clay when she heard the rumble of his black SUV coming down the driveway. She took a deep breath and pasted a half smile on her face as she watched him exit the vehicle and amble in her direction.

"Hey," he greeted with a wide smile, revealing the upper arch of his teeth. "How was your day, Jennie?" Clay wore a long-sleeved shirt that looked like it was made of the softest cotton. The light moss green colour drew Jennie's eye, as it was one of her favourites.

"Fine," she said, masking her true feelings, "but I'm pressed for time, Clay, so let's head over to the bluff. Maybe you can fill me in on your idea along the way."

Jennie felt her back teeth clench together, a habit she knew she needed to break. The white ridge visible on the inside of her left cheek indicated a serious concern, her dentist had warned.

As they approached the bluff, Clay extended his arms wide,

his expression bursting with enthusiasm. "This expansive, open space is perfect for what I have in mind," he declared with a broad grin. "There's plenty of room to spread out the equipment and take a run at it when the opportunity seems right."

"And what about the log fence?" asked Jennie. "Doesn't it get in the way?"

Clay chuckled. "I guess you haven't seen us in action. We glide right over it, at the best of times."

"You make it sound like there's room for error," Jennie said.

"Like anything." Clay replied. "But the accident rate in this sport is exceptionally low, and I've never had a serious mishap in all the 25 years I've been doing this."

He must have sensed Jennie's skepticism, despite her attempt to hide it. Clay stood tall, his shoulders squared confidently. "I can assure you, Jennie, I have exceptional glider control."

But Jennie's mind raced with questions, and she barely took a breath before unleashing them. "How often do you hold classes, Clay, and how many students are there per class?"

Clay opened his mouth as though to reply, an exercise in futility considering what followed.

"What time of day would you start? How long would each class last and what is the duration of the course? Do you hope to run courses back-to-back?"

Jennie's rapid-fire interrogation left no room for Clay to respond.

She surprised even herself, giving rise to her secret fear that she might be on the verge of a nervous breakdown. *I shouldn't have had that third cup of coffee.*

But Jennie couldn't seem to help herself. "What days of the week would you train? Do you work on stat holidays? Do you have insurance in case someone injures themselves on my property?"

Clay burst into laughter at the barrage of questions. "Well, I can see that you've put some serious thought into this," he said good-naturedly. "And I can easily answer all of your questions and more, given a bit of time," he added with a smile.

Before Jennie could interject, he quickly added, "Have you had supper yet?"

Jennie hesitated slightly before nodding her head vaguely and said, "Uh, yeah, I have." Another fib.

"Why don't we sit out on the veranda?" Jennie offered, thinking a change of scene might help her relax. "I can get you a coffee and a snack to tide you over if you like."

"I'd like that very much, Jen...may I call you Jen?

"My loved ones call me Jen, but I'll make an exception in your case," she laughed softly at her own joke, trying to appear somewhat grounded.

As they walked through the rocky, moss-laden terrain, Clay shared the funniest joke Jennie had heard in ages. Reflecting on the stress of the day, she knew she needed more laughter in her life, and humour seemed to come so easily to Clay.

I haven't laughed this much for a very long time, she said to herself, savouring the moment.

As they settled on the veranda, Clay answered all of Jennie's questions between mouthfuls of cheese, crackers, and grapes. He tried to assure her he knew what he was doing.

"I'm a P4 pilot, Advanced rated, and both a Senior HPAC Paragliding Instructor and a Tandem II Instructor."

Jennie attached little significance to the credentials, but she inferred they must be important.

"The season typically runs from April through October. Our down-time is when there's no wind, but we operate year-round, depending on the weather," explained Clay.

Jennie nodded, understanding the seasonal rhythm. "Oh, similar to my B&B," she remarked, finding a commonality in their business models.

Clay's expression lit up at Jennie's observation, finding reassurance in the parallel in case that somehow helped her decide in his favour. He smiled warmly at Jennie, his turquoise eyes accentuated by the blue and green throw pillows thoughtfully arranged on the chaise longue.

Clay continued confidently. "Of course, I'd want to have access to the area year-round, so I would cover costs for a yearly lease." Leaning forward, he rested his elbows on his knees, his hands folded together in anticipation.

"So, what do you think, Jen?" he asked, his eagerness palpable as he awaited her response.

Jennie was quick to respond. "Here's what I think, Clay. I'll be as direct with you as you've been with me."

She paused briefly, contemplating her words before revealing her true motivation for considering the deal.

"I'll be honest, I could use the extra income, especially during off-season at the B&B."

"And, you know," she continued, her voice tinged with uncertainty, "I had to think long and hard before starting this B&B largely because I didn't want to give up my privacy. Now, if I were to agree with your proposal, well, there'd be even more strangers tromping across my property at all hours of the day and in all seasons."

The more Jennie envisioned the consequences, the more uneasy she felt. "I mean, that's a lot to swallow, Clay." Jennie sighed deeply, her shoulders slumping as she contemplated the implications.

"I get it, Jen, but it's not as if we'd be coming close to your house." Clay stood up and gestured toward the area where the driveway intersected with the side road. "Look, I can make a trail way over there. I can even construct a parking area far from your driveway if you'd like."

Jennie thought about his idea. "No, to the separate parking area," she concluded. "There's plenty of room for parking by the side of the road just outside of the property."

She continued with confidence, well aware of her parameters. "And there's no need for you to make a trail. You and your entourage can simply come in along the fence line to the right of the driveway as you enter the property. That'll be the least intrusive way by far."

Jennie hoped she didn't sound unfriendly, but she had learned the importance of putting on her business hat and separating business from pleasure. Yet she had to admit that her interactions with Clay so far had been remarkably pleasurable.

"Agreed. Sounds like the perfect solution. So, is it a deal, then?" Clay's stunning turquoise eyes were wide with anticipation, a spark of hope dancing within.

But Jennie still was uncertain. "I may be overly cautious, but as a widow, I have to be."

"Yes," acknowledged Clay, "I met your husband Derrick years ago, and I'm so sorry for your loss."

Jennie felt her heart race. "Huh? You knew Derrick?"

"We belonged to the same hiking group when he was studying to be a private investigator."

Jennie raised her brows. "That was a long time ago, over 20 years, but I remember how much he loved hiking. I wish I'd joined him, but I always seemed to have too much else to do."

"It's never too late, Jen. I'd be happy to take you hiking up Mount Maxwell someday."

"That's kind of you, Clay, but these days I have to stick close to home." Jennie returned to the matter at hand. "Anyway, the biggest downside remains the invasion of privacy, but more important is the fact that I would have no control over who may come onto my property... who is looking at my house, at me, my mother, you know... surveying the scene." Jennie's pitch rose, perhaps higher than she would have preferred.

Clay nodded his head in agreement. "I understand completely, and I'm sure I'd feel the same way if I were in your situation. Those are legitimate concerns." He looked directly into Jennie's eyes, exuding empathy and captivating her with his sincere demeanour.

"But I promise you, Jen, I'll respect your privacy as much as I can, and I won't let anyone wander off-limits. I don't investigate everyone who signs up for lessons, but I can guarantee you that our focus will be on learning the skill of paragliding, not on casing your joint."

Pleased with Clay's reassuring response, Jennie smiled warmly. "Okay, I just wanted to be crystal clear about my concerns. I don't want there to be any misunderstandings between us."

"Gotcha. I'm all into clear communication," Clay reassured.

Clay's prolonged gaze made Jennie feel uncomfortable, prompting her to retreat inwardly. Sensing her reticence, he shifted gears and continued to promote his business, this time approaching it from a new angle.

"You may not have considered this potential benefit," he began in an upbeat tone, attempting to steer the conversation in a positive direction. "People seem fascinated watching paragliders. Once your property becomes known as a paragliding destination, enthusiasts will actively seek places to enjoy the spectacle."

"Oh, that seems to be an argument against your proposal," Jennie countered.

"It'll increase visibility for your B&B. If you're hoping to beat the competition, this may be your ticket," he suggested optimistically. Clay added, "One advantage of your site would be that there'd be no public interaction. That's one drawback of other sites, such as the one on Dallas Road in Victoria."

Jennie had a blank expression on her face as Clay added, " I mean, people could watch from a distance, but they wouldn't be allowed onto the training site."

Feeling the need for some space to mull over the conversation without the influence of Clay, Jennie excused herself. "I'll be right back. If you'd like a refill, the kitchen's this way," she offered, opening the main door to the house and gesturing toward the kitchen.

Clay followed her into the house, heading toward the kitchen with his coffee mug while Jennie made her way into her home office, closing the door behind her.

Sitting at the desk, Jennie couldn't shake the conflicting thoughts swirling in her mind. *If I agree to Clay's terms, will I only add to the stress I already have with the B&B? But will I have regrets if I turn down his offer?*

Jennie quickly devised a solution. *I'll lay it out clearly in the contract. Either of us can opt out without notice.*

Clay's account, of course, would have to be paid in full up to his departure, she decided, feeling a sense of relief at finding a compromise. Sitting for some time, weighing the pros and cons, she finally emerged from the office.

Joining Clay on the veranda, she declared, "I think we can work out something agreeable to us both."

Jennie presented Clay with her idea for an opt-out agreement, outlining the terms they had discussed. She assured him she would draw up the contract for his signature, and they shook hands amicably, sealing their agreement.

"Jennie, you won't regret it," Clay assured her with a warm smile. "I think it'll be good for both of us." Clay's pleasure was palpable. "How soon can we start?" he asked enthusiastically, his eagerness apparent in his tone.

Jennie gazed into Clay's eyes, momentarily thinking about his association with Derrick. In a way, Clay reminded Jennie of her former husband. *He seems to be a man of good character, like Derrick was; they were friends, after all.*

He seems forthright and fun-loving like Derrick was. Certainly, he's every bit as charming and handsome as my Derrick. Then she told herself not to be so silly. *This guy's like a hippie. Nothing at all like Derrick. I can't even imagine being in a serious relationship with Clay.*

After Clay left and Jennie felt satisfied that the breakfast room was ready for the first sitting, she allowed herself some self-care. She ran a hot bath, adding a few drops of lavender oil. As she settled into the tub, the soothing water enveloped her tired muscles, and a wave of deep relaxation washed over her.

Reflecting on their meeting, Jennie allowed herself a measure of excitement at what was to come, acknowledging the unexpected spark of attraction toward Clay. *He's a good-looking dude, even if he was late.*

RAIN PELTED DOWN EARLY the next morning, accompanied by a howling wind that rattled the windows, stirring Jennie from a much-needed sleep. With her restless mind replaying events from the day before and listing the tasks awaiting her today, she thought, *Might as well get up.*

Placing her bare feet onto the cold floorboards, she added a warm sweater to her standard attire of blue jeans and a T-shirt. Descending the long staircase, she was about to pass the home office when she heard a dripping sound. Oh, no, please, she muttered under her breath, dreading the possibility of a leak in the house.

Holding her breath, she cautiously peered into the office, almost afraid to look. Rushing to the bookshelf, she frantically removed batches of books, mostly from the top shelf to a dry spot on the floor. She knew better than to place soggy books on the oak desk unless she wanted watermarks.

Racing into the kitchen, she withdrew a yellow plastic pail from underneath the sink. Setting the pail on top of the bookshelf to collect the drips, she stared at the ceiling. The makeshift roof repair Derrick had carried out, but didn't get back to, couldn't withstand the force of this unusually heavy rainfall.

With both hands on her hips, Jennie sighed deeply, having no other choice than to call for expert help. Another unexpected expense. Another unexpected chore. She stooped down and collected the books one at a time, spreading the pages wide and fitting them over the wooden rungs of her portable clothes dryer, just as she and Derrick had done before.

Making herself some coffee, Jennie sat down at the kitchen table to research local roofers. Simple decision. A choice of two. He offered to come on an emergency basis.

With Kathleen staying at Alexa's apartment, it was Jennie's responsibility to gather the eggs and tend to the henhouse. Pushing her feet into her rain boots, she put on her raincoat and headed toward the henhouse with her wire egg basket. She raised her hood, reminding herself to keep a close eye on the drip pail on top of the bookshelf. The rain fell hard and fast.

At the end of the wood chip trail, as Jennie approached the door of the henhouse, she shrieked, frozen in place. A thin rat with what seemed like an extra-long tail scurried away from the feeding yard and under the nearby Berberis hedge. Her heart pounded inside her chest.

The rickety door to the feeding yard stuttered as she forced it open. She immediately noticed a gap dug under the fencing, likely the rat's entry point. Fearing what she might find in the chicken coop, she hesitated, bracing for whatever awaited her. As raindrops trickled down her bare hands, she noticed a slight tremble. Glancing down at her footwear, she couldn't shake the image of rodents scurrying over the top of her rubber boots.

Jennie forced herself to move forward toward the coop. Inside, she counted 11 hens, six of them in their nests. Setting down the basket, she headed back outside, scanning the area for the twelfth hen. It didn't take long before she spotted white feathers scattered in an area at the end of the hedge.

Jennie's first thought was that Kathleen would be upset. Her mother had made pets of the poultry, assigning a name to each one. Her second thought was, *Oh, no, not more rats.*

Her mind raced with thoughts of how to secure the hen yard against persistent rodents. *If they can dig under the fence, how can I possibly stop them?* Jennie could feel her skin uncomfortably wet above the zipper of her coat, which was unprotected by the meagre peak of her rain hood.

This is not defeat; it's nothing you can't handle, she told herself firmly, determined to push back the encroaching sense of overwhelm. Yet Jennie could feel herself tinkering on the edge of instability, threatening to engulf her. Taking a moment to steady herself, she took in a deep breath and focussed intently on the vibrant, pink blooms of the peony bush by the granary.

Feeling a little more grounded, Jennie returned to the chicken coop, entering with caution. Not finding any long-tailed intruders, Jennie felt a sense of relief. She now understood why all of her hens stayed put in their nesting boxes that morning. Carefully reaching under the hens, she retrieved 18 eggs, mostly white.

Trudging wearily up the chip trail toward the house, she noticed the roofer's van pull in and park on the edge of her circular driveway. With a sense of urgency, she hurried to greet him and quickly led him through the kitchen entrance to the home office, throwing off her dripping raincoat and leaving it draped over a kitchen chair. Hoisting the egg basket onto the kitchen counter, she worried she'd be short of time to prepare for the 7:00 breakfast seating.

Pointing out areas of leakage, Jennie and the roofer, Dan, discussed the needed repairs.

Leaving him to do his job, Jennie dashed upstairs, feeling a surge of emotions as she struggled to hold back tears. Time was of the essence, and despite the challenges of the morning, she was determined to meet her responsibilities.

BY THE TIME Jennie busied herself in the kitchen, bustling to kick-start the morning breakfast, she noticed the rain had finally stopped. The wind still raged outside, and she knew that anything not securely anchored would likely blow away. But she had to focus on breakfast, and the woman beckoning for her attention.

As Jennie approached the table designated for Room Three guests, the female guest, sitting with her male companion, launched into her story without hesitation.

"You know," she began, her hair neatly in place despite the weather, "everything here is perfect, just like the brochure on the ferry promised." She spoke firmly but politely at first.

Scraping her chair back against the wood floor, she rose from her seat, her demeanour shifting slightly. "But I'll be honest with you Jennie," she continued, leaning in close and lowering her voice to a whisper as she spoke directly into Jennie's ear like a schoolgirl telling secrets. "I simply can't tolerate rats, and I spotted three of them."

Jennie summoned a warm smile, momentarily averting her gaze and addressing the woman standing before her.

"I apologize," she began earnestly. "This is a recent issue for us here at Cliffhouse, but believe me, the problem will be short-lived, I promise."

Although sounding confident, Jennie secretly hoped that she could indeed fulfill her promise.

"Good," the woman replied, settling back into her chair with a slight frown. "I certainly hope so, because it changes everything for me."

She delicately adjusted her delicate chiffon scarf, which had slipped to the side as she had whispered in Jennie's ear.

The woman's words had pierced Jennie's heart. It was one thing to deal with problems behind the scenes, but a guest complaint threatened her reputation as a super host, something she had worked tirelessly to build.

In a hushed tone, Jennie turned away from guests seated at Table #1 and discreetly asked the woman where exactly she had spotted the rats…three of them. *Ugh.* The thought made Jennie's stomach churn with disgust.

The woman pushed away her breakfast plate, her expression troubled. "I took a morning stroll toward the barn," she began. "The door was open, so I peeked inside, and there they were, feasting on who-knows-what?"

The guest paused before asking a question. "Do you happen to keep chickens?"

"Uh, yes, I do," Jennie admitted, trying to keep her tone

neutral despite the rising unease. "Hence, the farm-fresh eggs."

Jennie hoped her response didn't come across as defensive. She knew she had little choice but to offer a second apology.

"Once again, I'm sorry you had to witness that," Jennie said, her tone genuine as she sought to convey empathy. "I only became aware of the issue myself a few nights ago. Please understand; this is a working farm."

Stop taking the defensive and don't sound condescending, Jennie admonished herself.

With a renewed smile, Jennie continued with as much warmth as she could muster. "But I completely understand your concern, and I share it wholeheartedly. I want you to know that I'm taking every step necessary to address the issue promptly."

Pausing for a moment, Jennie couldn't help but worry about the impact this incident might have on her guests' perception of Cliffhouse by the Sea. Worse yet, she worried they might leave a critical review.

"I assure you, the next time you visit, it won't be an issue." *Don't make false promises,* Jennie scolded herself.

Jennie's mind raced with conflicting thoughts. *Should I offer a refund for their one-night stay? Even if I did, would it dissuade them from giving a bad review? I can't afford to give up the night's rent. Besides, she wouldn't have seen the rats if she hadn't nosed her way into the barn.*

"Now," Jennie interjected quickly, eager to create a diversion from the uncomfortable topic, "can I offer you another cup of coffee? Perhaps a few muffins to take on the road?"

"I think I'm done," the disgruntled woman replied curtly, her frustration apparent as she pushed her chair back with unnecessary force. Her male companion mirrored her actions, remaining expressionless throughout the exchange.

Swiftly, they pulled open the solid wood inner door, then pushed open the screen door, braving the wind as they left the breakfast room without another word.

Jennie sighed, feeling a mixture of relief and apprehension. She watched as they linked arms in solidarity, crossing the veranda and heading toward a shiny black Lincoln.

Jennie had a sinking feeling that she would never again see their vehicle in her driveway. Her apprehension grew as she prepared to face the fallout from a potential negative review.

Jennie said a silent prayer. *Please don't ruin my 5-star rating.*

As she gathered the dishes from Table #1, a movement near the entrance to her property drew Jennie's attention.

Squinting, she recognized Clay and three other people hauling paragliding equipment across the field along the fence line. A spark of hope flickered within her—a silver lining to an otherwise trying day.

They'll soon beat down a path leading directly to the launch site, thought Jennie. *If there's one good thing that comes out of this god-forsaken day, maybe this is it.*

CHAPTER 14

After tidying the breakfast room and kitchen, Jennie found herself with some spare time before the scheduled changeovers. Bundling up in her coat, she zipped it high under her chin and secured her hair under a knitted hat. With a purposeful stride, she located Dan diligently working on the roof over the home office. "It's taking a while up there, Dan," she called out, raising her voice to be heard over the wind. "Is everything okay?"

"Oh, yeah, it's fine, ma'am," Dan reassured, his voice carrying down from the roof. "I had to go to town to get a special piece, but I'll finish here in about ten minutes."

Jennie cringed at the word 'ma'am', a reminder of her advancing years, then chuckled at her reaction. *What else would it be? I'm hardly a 'miss' anymore.* Still, the incessant bombardment of ads targeting aging women with sagging jowls, age spots, wrinkles, and other so-called imperfections apparently to be avoided at all costs drew her attention.

"Okay, just knock on the kitchen door when you're done,"

she called back, pushing aside her momentary reflections as she turned to head back inside.

Removing her outdoor clothing, Jennie hung them neatly in the hallway before realizing she'd forgotten to eat breakfast herself. Strolling to the kitchen, she considered her options, feeling uninspired by the thought of cooking yet another egg.

Glancing at the mixing bowl, she noticed that there wasn't any more pancake batter. Opting for simplicity, she poured some boxed granola into a bowl, followed by a good measure of almond milk. She sliced half a banana on top and then drizzled a measured amount of maple syrup over a dollop of organic, unflavoured yogurt, creating a simple yet satisfying breakfast.

Jennie's mouth was full when Dan knocked firmly on the kitchen door as if he were using a hammer. Jennie was about to Google how to keep rats out of the henhouse and the barn. Through the window, she gestured for Dan to come in. "Sorry, I was just having a bite," she said apologetically.

"No worries, ma'am," Dan replied, placing the thin paper invoice on the table in front of her.

Jennie picked up the invoice, her eyes immediately sweeping to the final total.

"Maybe I should've gotten an estimate," she said weakly to Dan.

"Even if you had, ma'am, I'm pretty sure you'd have gone ahead, anyway," he replied, his tone matter-of-fact.

"You can't fool around with this kind of thing. I mean, the patch-up job that was done beforehand may have worked for a bit, but it was eventually going to leak again. Honestly, I don't think any band-aid-type kind of repair would have worked this time," he explained.

"I see," Jennie replied, absorbing Dan's explanation. "Uh, do you offer any kind of payment plan?" she ventured.

"I'm a private business, ma'am, and this is my only source of income." His words hung in the air as he appeared deep in thought.

The longer he remained silent, the more Jennie became convinced he wouldn't agree to a payment plan. She braced herself for disappointment, preparing to consider other options for handling the unexpected expense.

"But, since this was an emergency repair and therefore a higher bill, I can offer you 50% now and 50% by the end of next month, if that helps."

Jennie's smile brightened at Dan's unexpected offer. "That helps immensely," she replied gratefully, knowing her bookings would cover the 50/50 split.

"I'll write you a cheque for half and be right back. Can I get you a coffee?"

Dan nodded appreciatively. "Sure, I could use a cup, thanks."

With a sense of relief, Jennie hurried inside to fetch her chequebook and prepare a fresh cup of coffee for Dan. As she headed into the kitchen, she said over her shoulder, "And if you know of anyone looking for a B&B, please mention Cliffhouse by the Sea."

As they wrapped up their business, Jennie accompanied Dan to his truck, noting that the wind had calmed considerably.

Jennie's thoughts wandered to Clay and his student, wondering if they were still paragliding. But the looming task of starting the changeovers pulled her back to the business at hand.

Reminding herself that all four guest rooms needed to be

prepared for the new arrivals by 4:00 pm., she waved goodbye to Dan and hurried back inside to begin the process.

Pausing briefly as she passed by the hall mirror, Jennie glimpsed her reflection. Areas of darkness had formed below her eyes, and a distinct red rim underscored her lower lids, evidence of the stress and exhaustion she had been feeling.

Her laugh lines seemed more noticeable than ever before. Though she had always appreciated the natural silver highlights in her hair, today they appeared more grey than silver, accentuating her fatigue.

With a sigh, Jennie forced herself to look away from her reflection. There was work to be done, guests to attend to, and little time to dwell on her appearance. She squared her shoulders and continued her tasks, determined to fill her responsibilities at Cliffhouse with grace and efficiency.

The next day, Jennie promised herself she would take a proper lunch break. *Maybe I'll go see what this paragliding thing is all about.*

Slapping together a simple cheese and lettuce sandwich, assembled with homemade bread and mayo, she tucked it into her bag before setting off through the fields toward the clifftop.

After just a few steps, the fresh air, and she had to admit, the prospect of witnessing Clay at work, lifted Jennie's spirits, providing a welcome break from the demands of running Cliffhouse.

Clay's commanding voice carried over the wind. "You, as the pilot in command of your aircraft, are solely responsible and accountable for the outcome of your flight. Just remember to keep a safe distance from each other, and remember the Right is Right Rule: The pilot with the ridge on his or her right has the right of way."

Not wanting to disrupt the activity, Jennie found a secluded spot just inside the log fencing where she could observe without getting in the way. As she headed toward the spot, Clay, at least she thought that was Clay, gave her a wave, and she waved back. Amid helmets, goggles, and backpacks, they all looked alike, she thought.

From her vantage point sitting on top of a grassy mound, Jennie took in the breathtaking scenery while enjoying the spectacle of one of the paragliders soaring through the sky. It was the perfect opportunity to unwind and immerse herself in the beauty of nature, if only for a short while.

Feeling somewhat rejuvenated after lunch, Jennie headed back to the house to finish her laundry. No one had asked for an early check-in, so she didn't have to rush.

After refreshing the flowers in the guest rooms, she planned to greet the new guests as they arrived, provided there were no further emergencies.

As Jennie waited for the pest control experts to arrive, she felt anxious. She had instructed them to park discreetly behind the barn, wary of any potential negative impact on her guests' experience should they see the advertising on the pest control vehicle.

Deep down, Jennie recognized that the health and safety of her guests was her number one priority, with the preservation of her hard-earned, five-star reputation a close second.

As requested, the pest control people arrived promptly at 1:00, a time that fell comfortably between check-out and check-in times for guests. Jennie followed the white van, its sides featuring a giant rat outlined in black, to its parking spot behind the barn.

With a sense of determination, she greeted the pest control experts and led them to the areas of concern, ready to tackle the problem head-on.

Leading the two men to the henhouse, she pointed out the gap beneath the chicken-wire fence. Together, they crafted an agreeable plan to set live traps instead of resorting to poison. The team committed to working over the next few days to seal any areas where rats were gaining access to the henhouse but acknowledged the challenge of replicating that process in the barn. They said it was likely chicken feed that initially attracted the rodents.

"Hey, Jen," a male voice shouted from the distance.

Looking toward the clifftop, Jennie spotted Clay tramping across the field in her direction. Thinking of her reflection in the hall mirror, she couldn't help but feel anxious about her appearance as Clay drew near.

"One of my students lost his phone and wondered if anyone had turned it in to you," Clay announced as he approached Jennie.

Jennie felt a wave of exhaustion wash over her with the thought of another issue to deal with. She felt as if she wasn't even present in the moment, but mumbled something about not having seen the phone. Her depletion wasn't hard to miss.

"Hey, I'm sorry to bother you, Jen," Clay said, his kind eyes meeting hers. "But I wanted to check in with you." He stopped talking, waiting for her response.

"Why's that, Clay?" she asked simply, her expression devoid of emotion.

"I'll tell you the truth, Jen," he said, his voice full of concern. "I can see that you're having a rough time, and I've noticed that you seem stressed out lately."

The last thing Jennie wanted was to feel like she was under scrutiny. "How do you know all this?" she asked, reining in her indignation.

"I notice things, that's all," Clay replied calmly. "The pest control truck this afternoon and the guy on the roof this morning. I know how things can add up when you're a homeowner. I'm one myself."

"Yeah," Jennie allowed, her tone softening. "Things have a way of snow-balling, don't they?" Her lips curved into half a smile as she gazed out toward the horizon, evading Clay's concerned eyes.

"That's a good way to describe it, Jen," Clay agreed. He tapped lightly behind her right shoulder and shifted his stance, bringing them face-to-face.

Jennie wasn't used to physical contact with a male other than her son Nick, and she hadn't seen him since last Christmas.

"You know, it's probably not the best time to ask," he said warmly, "but I'd like to help, if you'll let me." He smiled gently, his gaze softening as he locked eyes with Jennie.

Jennie wasn't used to receiving such concern from a stranger. A stranger who was male. A male who wasn't Derrick.

She remained quiet for a moment, fighting against her instinct to reject his offer with a polite "No, thanks, I'm fine," followed by a quick exit.

But Jennie could not deny the overwhelming sense of defeat that permeated her being. Summoning all her courage, she looked into Clay's eyes, intending to speak, but a flood of tears betrayed her anguish before she could utter a word.

Hastily wiping them away with her hands, she was surprised when Clay opened his arms wide, offering her a comforting embrace.

For a moment, Jennie hesitated, her pride warring against her need for comfort. With a deep breath, she finally yielded.

Jennie felt the strength of his muscles as Clay tenderly drew her in close, enveloping her in his arms.

"It's okay, Jen, go ahead and cry. Cry it all out, there's no one here but us."

Settling into the warmth of Clay's body and the strength of his physique, Jennie felt a comfort she hadn't experienced since her time with Derrick.

Startled by a voice calling out to them, Jennie gently freed herself from Clay's embrace when she saw a young woman rushing toward them, her voice urgent. "Excuse me," she shouted. "Your horse is out."

Without a word, Jennie sprang into action, racing toward the corral and spotting her palomino mare galloping around the open fields. She noticed Clay dashing like an Olympian toward the entrance to her driveway, a distance away. Fortunately, with Clay patrolling the driveway area, the horse was unlikely to head in that direction.

Reaching the gate at the bottom of the driveway, Clay closed it shut, securing it with the attached metal chain. Panting, he headed up the driveway toward the open fields. As he approached Jennie, he asked confidently, "Can you get some grain?"

Jennie nodded and ran back toward the granary while Clay monitored the mare while approaching a couple standing by their car parked in the driveway.

"We just drove in and saw this beauty galloping free," explained a young woman dressed in red shorts and a white sleeveless tee, "but that didn't seem right, so I thought I'd better let someone know. We were hoping for an early check-in, that's all."

"Thank you for letting us know," Clay replied kindly. "Now,

if you don't mind, will you please get back into your car until we get this animal back into the corral? Horses can be skittish and easily spooked, so we want a calm environment. Nothing to freak her out."

Nodding agreeably, the couple left their car doors ajar, probably to avoid the slamming noise.

By now, Jennie had returned with a feedbag full of oats. "Perfect," said Clay, reaching for it, their hands brushing together momentarily. In that fleeting touch, a surge of warmth and connection passed between them, stirring deeply within Jennie.

Clay pushed the feedbag back to her. "Jen, the horse knows you, not me, so you'd be the one to offer her some grain. Once she takes some of it, you can stroll into the corral and I'll close the gate."

Clay's confidence resonated with Jennie, evoking memories of the harmonious partnership she'd shared with Derrick, seamlessly tackling whatever challenges came their way.

"Music," Jennie cheerfully called to the mare that had been her pet since she was a foal. "Come on, girl," she said, rattling the oats.

Clay stood well back from the gate so as not to spook the mare as Jennie continued coaxing.

"Come on, Music; come on, girl."

Jennie hoped that Music would be back in the corral before any more guests came, as that could present new challenges. The gate was closed for now, but anyone could figure out how to un-loop the chain and open it.

After a few more laps in the open fields, Music made her way to Jennie and the oats. Clay's plan appeared to be working. When Jennie led her mare to the far side of the corral, Clay walked over and secured the corral gate.

"I must have forgotten to lock the gate after feeding her

this morning," Jennie said, furrowing her brow, "although I really don't remember leaving it unlocked."

"Doesn't matter now, Jen; she's safe and sound with your loving TLC," he reassured her. "And now, you'll probably want to attend to your guests," he added with a supportive smile, gently nudging Jenny forward.

"Clay, I can't thank you enough." She reached out and lightly brushed her fingertips against the back of his hand.

"Listen," she continued, "would you like to come for supper tomorrow night? I honestly feel exhausted after today. It was a doozy," she added with a tired smile.

"Jen, I'd love to, but I'm not available tomorrow night, and I refuse to put you to any more work. Instead, I'd like to invite you to go kayaking with me on Sunday. Is that possible?"

Jennie smiled gratefully. "That's so kind, Clay, and I truly appreciate your offer. The trouble is...I have to be available 24/7 in case there are any issues here with the B&B."

Clay spoke patiently, his tone reassuring. "I promise you, Jen, there are at least two good reasons that it's okay for you to take a few hours to relax," he countered.

"One is that this is the age of digital communications," he said with a hint of amusement. "Your cell phone number is on your business card; anyone can reach you as long as you keep your phone charged. Another reason is that we live on a small island and can be anywhere within minutes."

Jennie chuckled at the seemingly obvious reasons Clay presented. "Ah, I guess it's no different from when I visit my kids for a bit. I don't know why I got so wound up over obligations that I was afraid to leave."

Clay's eyes responded with a smile. "Sunday, then? I don't have classes that day, so we're good. How 'bout I pick you up at ten?"

"I can make a picnic... ," Jennie offered, but before she

could finish, Clay cut in, gently placing his hand on her arm, emphasizing his point.

"Just bring a water bottle, a hat, and yourself, please. I'll handle lunch." Then he added, "If you have some water shoes, pack those along too."

Jennie couldn't deny the unexpected thrill that coursed through her at Clay's gentle touch. *This is crazy. There's no way I'm getting involved in a serious relationship with Clay. I'm just not.*

CHAPTER 15

Sunday morning arrived quickly, and the weather was unusually warm for March. Jennie observed Clay's SUV as it rolled down the driveway, two kayaks securely strapped to the roof. *He's actually on time*, she thought to herself, smiling.

As she approached, she felt a thrilling sensation in her stomach. She was determined not to over-analyze why he'd asked her out or why she felt awkward stepping into his SUV with her water shoes in one hand and water bottle in the other.

One thing she knew for certain: She owed it to herself to break the punishing routine she adhered to, even if only for a few hours. Jennie had slept soundly, as she often did when exhausted. Today, she was ready for some fun and she hoped to make the most of her precious few hours of downtime.

"Morning, Jen. I thought we'd go to Wallace Island. Ever been there?" Clay asked cheerfully.

Fastening her seatbelt, she replied, "No, haven't been to Wallace Island, but it sounds wonderful. You could tell me we're going to Lower Slobbovia, and I'd say we can't get there soon enough."

"Ha," laughed Clay. "Where is that, anyway?"

"As I recall," said Jennie, "it doesn't even exist, but I think it's meant to portray a place that's backward and unenlightened."

"Sounds fascinating," Clay responded with a broad smile as he circled the turnaround, drove down the driveway, and headed toward Hudson Point, where they'd launch the kayaks.

As they cruised along the winding road, Clay broke the silence. "Jen, it's clear things have been tough lately, even from the brief snapshot I've seen of your life these past few days. If you feel like unloading once we arrive, I'm here to listen. But hey, if you'd rather leave it all behind and soak up today, count me in for that adventure, too."

Jennie pondered his words for a moment before responding. "That's so kind of you, Clay; thank you. I'll admit that I'm desperate to get away from it all, so today I'm going to pretend that I'm leaving behind one world and travelling to a different world. So that would be a 'No' to talking about anything to do with that world back there." She raised her chin, affirming her choice.

Parking at Hudson Point, Clay unloaded the kayaks. Looking ahead, he remarked on the calmness of the water. The low tide had exposed an extensive beach, making it easy to launch. They stuffed their supplies in the kayak cubbies, put on their water shoes and life jackets, and pushed off into the sea.

Carrying their backpacks over rocky terrain, they trekked through a forested area and reached the campground at Chivers Point on the island's northwest tip. Discovering an unoccupied picnic table, they carefully set down their belongings on its surface.

With a gentle touch, Clay took hold of Jennie's hand and spoke softly, "May I lead you to see the view?"

Jennie's felt a flutter in her stomach when Clay's hand intertwined with hers. Though his gesture initially seemed bold, she couldn't deny the warmth it brought her. She welcomed the attention, relished his charisma, and to her surprise, found comfort in the companionship of a man after such a long time.

Clay pointed out Trincomali Channel and across to Galiano Island. "Ever been to Galiano, Jen?"

"Yes, I attended an arts festival there a few years back. I love the view from the ridge."

"One of my favourite places to stay," said Clay, "and one of the few places where I don't bring along camping equipment."

"You mean you sleep under the stars?" teased Jennie.

Clay chuckled, "My survival skills are pretty top-notch, Jen, thanks to some of my native friends but, no, I meant that on Galiano Island I stay in a small cabin built on the side of a cliff."

"Oh, sounds fascinating, Clay. Maybe you could build me one of those, and I can get someone else to run the B&B," she laughed. "Or, better yet, scrap the B&B and use the money I get from renting the cliff-side cabin to pay the overdue bills and sail off to Hawaii."

"Good job not talking about work, Jen," Derrick remarked, causing both of them to chuckle. "Come over here," Clay invited, guiding her to the shore. I want to show you what's lurking in these waters."

Massive oysters lay atop the rocks. Clay wore neoprene boots, and Jennie was glad she had located her water shoes in an old snorkel bag she and Derrick used to take on trips to the tropical islands.

"Look at that huge starfish," marvelled Jen. "Such a beautiful shade of purple." Upon closer inspection, Jennie spotted two more—one red and one orange. Her creative mind imagined a watercolour painting or a starfish embossed on a clay soap dish.

"You know," said Clay, "crabs are so plentiful here, you can pick them up in your hands, or even metal tongs. Some of my friends can even pick them up barehanded. There's a fantastic array of marine life here, Jen. I forgot about the mussels and rockfish."

Time seemed to evaporate as Jennie lost herself in a new world filled with natural wonders. She reflected on the island's beauty, realizing that despite living in paradise, one often overlooked the opportunity to truly appreciate it.

Clay glanced at the time display on his fitness watch and declared it was time to eat.

Removing the lunch he'd packed from the double layer of dry bags, he arranged it on a colourful piece of oilcloth they'd spread across the picnic table. He'd selected an array of local cheeses and wine, a buttered baguette, thinly sliced prosciutto, and crispy-looking purple grapes.

As he poured the white wine, Clay remarked, "I've seen some spectacular sunsets from here, you know. Maybe we can enjoy the sunset together sometime, Jen."

Feeling the romantic nuance of Clay's comment, Jennie chose not to reply directly. Instead, she smiled pleasantly and said, "This looks so inviting, Clay. Great job. I feel blessed to be here with you today."

Lifting her glass, she toasted Clay and asked, "Do you think we have time to hike the trails here?"

"We have time, and don't worry, we also have a cell phone

connection. I checked because I figured you might be concerned," Clay said, giving Jennie a reassuring squeeze.

After lunch, they gathered their remaining supplies and stored them in the metal food cache while they went hiking.

Jennie felt a profound sense of freedom as she walked along the well-worn forest trails and up the highest points on the island. The warmth of the sun on her bare skin seemed to replenish her soul. The air was clear, and some distance ahead, she could see a couple of adults with a child and a small dog.

Jennie noticed herself panting by the time they reached the top of the hill. "I'm so out of shape," she commented to Clay. "You know, I used to play tennis and attend yoga classes regularly. I was in pretty good shape back then," she reflected.

They found a grassy area between the rocks and sat down on a hilltop looking back toward Sunrise Island. They were both quiet for a while, and Jennie couldn't help but notice how comfortable she was sitting in silence with Clay.

Acknowledging that it's rare to find such ease in shared quietness with another person, Jennie savoured the moments, sensing that Clay also embraced this special time together.

"I've been checking the wind," Clay said. "When it's warm and clear like this, you have to be careful. Strong winds from the north can affect the return trip but, don't worry, I'm on top of it," he reassured.

"Right now," said Jennie, "I feel like I don't care if we can't make it back." Feeling sleepy from the wine and the warm sun, she lay back on the grass, her hands interlaced behind her head.

"Looks like mission accomplished then," said Clay, smiling down at her.

Jennie closed her eyes against the bright sun and imagined herself lying on the beach in Hawaii. She sensed the replenishing rays of the sun seep into the layers of her skin.

When Clay's soft lips touched hers ever so gently, she startled and abruptly pushed herself to sit upright, gasping and confused.

"What the...? I let my guard down for a moment, and this happens." Her guard, momentarily lowered, left her startled by the unexpected intimacy.

Clay recoiled, his hand dropping from her shoulder as he looked down, apologetic. "I'm so sorry, Jen. That was presumptuous of me," he murmured. "Truly sorry. You looked so peaceful, so beautiful there..."

"I was at peace, Clay, but not anymore," Jennie confessed, her brow furrowing as her thoughts raced. After briefly pausing, she continued, "I want you to understand that I'm not looking for a relationship. I apologize if I led you to believe otherwise."

Clay's voice softened. "I understand, Jen. I really am sorry," he repeated quietly.

Jennie's tone grew gentle as she responded. "I love what we did today, Clay. Please don't misunderstand. And I'd love to spend time with you when it's good for both of us," she continued. "It's just that I don't have much time these days, as you know."

In the deepest part of her heart, Jennie worried that her abrupt reaction had been unwarranted. *He's a good man. What's wrong with me?*

As Jennie pondered her inner turmoil, Clay reached out, taking her hand and helping her up.

"I'd like to chat with you sometime," he suggested, "and see if I can help you streamline things a bit. You know, so you don't have to work so hard."

Jennie scoffed at the idea. "When you run a B&B, you're on call 24/7, and being on my own, everything that happens is my responsibility. It weighs on me, sure, but I'm up for it because I have to be."

She immediately regretted saying that. It sounded whiny, she thought, and she didn't want to come across that way to anyone.

"I get it, Jen; I do. But if you're up for discussing viable alternatives sometime, you may find that I have some ideas worth considering. Just sayin'," he added with a smile.

"All right, Clay," Jennie added cheerily. "What have I got to lose? I'll make supper for us this week and we can chat then if you like. How about Tuesday at six?"

Tuesday at six arrived before Jennie was ready. She had hurried to the village right after the breakfast clean-up to return a jar of homemade marmalade. Unfortunately, the seal broke, causing it to leak all over the other items and her reusable bag. With no time to spare, she'd had to clean the sticky mess and hand wash the bag, pegging it to the clothesline to dry.

Her face turned red with embarrassment when the grocery store cashier told her that her friend Margie had made the preserves. Had she known, she never would have returned the jar.

Driving back to Cliffhouse, faster than she normally would, Jennie had a chat with herself. *Who in their right mind would bother to return one jar of marmalade in the middle of such a busy day when it wasn't even that important?*

Despite her preoccupation with the marmalade, Jennie couldn't help but notice that Spanish broom had invaded so much more landscape than it had the previous year. The familiar bright yellow flowers of the pesky but cheery shrubbery overtook the landscape on both sides of the road.

Someone should form a group to help rid the island of this pest. Not me, she promised herself. I can't take on one more thing.

Regretfully, she'd already bowed out of baking pies for the community supper. She had stopped attending meetings of the Potter's Guild, she no longer attended yoga classes, and tennis doubles came to a halt when she lost Derrick. She volunteered in the Shriner's food truck as long as she could, but that eventually went by the wayside along with so many activities she used to enjoy.

The last Potter's Guild meeting she had attended did not go well. She wished she could erase the memory, but it remained vivid, and she kept replaying it in the movie theatre of her mind. When she raised her hand to make a suggestion, all eyes fixed on her. She explained that to follow the accepted protocol for business meetings, they needed to have a written record of the proceedings at each meeting.

Complete silence engulfed the room. Still standing, she heard mumbling among some members and caught what seemed to be sympathetic smiles from others. After the meeting, Bev took her aside and asked if everything was all right. That was the last meeting Jennie attended.

And then there was the Shriner's Club. While serving burgers one day at the Saturday Market, Jennie tactfully suggested to the cook that the burgers would be juicier if she didn't press the spatula into the burger patty while it was cooking.

"It squeezes out the moisture," she said, peering at the grill. "Do you see how the juices run out?" asked Jennie pointing to a pool of now-dried meat juice, "leaving the meat rather dry?"

The Shriners served the best burgers and fries on the

island, as far as Jennie was concerned. She didn't want their reputation tarnished for lack of a simple improvement.

The cook listened politely, then returned to cooking the burgers the same as she always had.

Undaunted, Jennie persisted, suggesting that they switch to grapeseed oil for frying because it wasn't carcinogenic at high heat levels.

But, no. The cook felt insulted and unappreciated, she said when asked why she no longer wanted to volunteer. At least she stayed until closing that day so they wouldn't be without a cook.

"My mistake," Jennie offered when the manager asked to hear her version of the story. Even though she knew she was right, she also knew that volunteer help was not always easy to find.

"Bring her back. You'll need her because I really can't spare the time to volunteer my services here any longer." She removed her apron and left the food truck for the last time. *What was I thinking?*

Jennie vividly recalled the rock-hard sensation in the pit of her stomach after that incident. Now avoiding buying food from the Shriner's truck, Jennie knew she was only hurting herself.

Aware of her mother's frustration, Kyla asked, "Mom, why not stick with selling pottery at the market? Everyone loves your flower bowls," she added, attempting to be encouraging.

Jennie had started teaching Kyla how to make clay pots on her pottery wheel, but that was while Derrick was still alive. Now that Jennie wasn't available to help, Kyla grew more frustrated trying it on her own. When she watched the wet clay collapse in on itself too many times, she quit.

And the last time Jennie was in her pottery studio was when she forced herself to make an urn to hold Derrick's ashes.

~

As she approached her driveway, Jennie heard the melodic sound of her cell phone ringing where it rested, face up, on the passenger seat. Despite being pressed for time, she turned into the driveway and stopped the car when she saw Bev's name appear on the display screen.

Shifting the gear to park, she settled into the call. "Bev," she said, feeling her neck and shoulder tension relax. "You probably don't know it, but your call is the highlight of my day so far."

With a voice as smooth as honey, Bev's warm, upbeat tone felt like home to Jennie. They could tell each other anything without fear of judgement. Jennie needed that, especially these days.

"That's always good to hear, Jen, and I think I can make your day even brighter." Bev launched right into it. "The girls and I are planning a trip to Europe in June," she said excitedly, "and we hope you can join us."

Jennie sat in silence for a moment, reminiscing about her old friend group sipping local wine at a small round table in an outdoor café in Paris, and cycling through the Tuscan vineyards before indulging in the best risotto ever, and buying a case of sumptuous Italian red to bring home.

"It breaks my heart to say no, dear friend, but June is busy with tourists, gardening, and farm maintenance. So, as much as I would love, love, love to go with all of you," Jen said, "I have obligations that I must honour. I'm sorry, Bev."

When they finished their conversation, Jennie sat alone in her vehicle, tears welling in her eyes.

As Jennie drove the length of the driveway toward her house, she envisioned Derrick mowing the lawn. Such images seemed to appear particularly when she felt stressed, she noted.

Kisses back to you, my love. Jennie blinked, clearing the tears from her eyes.

IN THE HOUSE, Jennie placed her new jar of marmalade on the shelf in the kitchen pantry, where she stored all of her preserves. Then she prepared to do the changeovers. There was only one for today, as the others had booked two and three days in a row.

Picking up her blue plastic laundry basket, she headed toward the kitchen door when her phone rang again. This time, it was Alexa.

Kathleen was ready to come home, Alexa said, and she agreed to drive her the next day. Alexa quietly implied to Jennie that she was ready to reclaim her own space by then.

"Yes, as much as you love someone, Lexi, it's nice to get back to normal after having visitors. And I miss having Mom around, not only for her company and spirit, but because I truly miss her help."

Changing the subject, Jennie asked, "Have you talked with Nick lately?"

"Yes, in fact, Kyla, Grandma, and I took him out for his birthday dinner last weekend. Dragged him away from his new girlfriend for a few hours," she laughed.

Jennie slapped one hand over her forehead and gasped. She cherished family celebrations. Hand-drawn hearts encircled the dates of every birthday, every holiday, and every special family event throughout the year on her calendar. Now she wondered if using her digital calendar might have alerted her to Nick's birthday. *Something else to figure out.*

"Lexi, I can't believe I forgot his birthday." She set her laundry basket on the floor, pulled out a chair, and slumped at the kitchen table.

"It's okay, Mom; we all know you have a lot on your plate. Please don't fret; we took good care of him."

After the call with Alexa ended, Jennie tried calling Nick, but there was no answer. She sent him a text, asking if he could come home next weekend. She would make his favourite dish, barbecued ribs, and his favourite angel food cake from an old family recipe. *How could he resist?*

Jennie resumed her chores, finishing in time to check in an older couple who lived on the island but wanted an easy getaway. When Jennie introduced herself, the woman cut her short.

"We know who you are. Your B&B runs like clockwork, they say, so we thought this would be the one to try," she said with smiling eyes.

"Thank you, kindly. I hope I meet your expectations," Jennie replied, grateful she'd replaced that jar of marmalade after all.

Time was short now. Jennie would have to plan supper after she showered. She had an hour and a half before Clay would arrive, provided he came on time.

Jennie visualized the contents of her fridge. Roasted chicken left over from last week, fresh tomatoes and cucumbers, asparagus well past its time. (*Why didn't I throw it out?*) and a bag of organic carrots. She pictured the contents of her freezer. Vegetarian pizza, pre-made from the grocery store, on sale for $3.00. Edamame. A variety of meat frozen solid.

～

As her thirsty towel soaked up most of the moisture from her hair, Jennie leaned against the edge of the bed, crossed her arms, and released a deep sigh. *I'm so tired of rushing.*

Wrapped in her cozy terry bathrobe, she lay on her back across the bed, indulging in a head-to-toe stretch. Soon, she slipped into a deep sleep, oblivious to the first round of phone chimes.

Groggily, she intercepted the second set of chimes, abruptly realizing she had dozed off when she couldn't afford to.

"Clay, I'm so, so sorry. Where are you right now? On the veranda?"

"Yep."

Jennie threw on a clean baby blue sweatsuit, pushed her hair away from her face, and hurried into the hall, down the stairs, and onto the veranda in her bare feet.

She was not expecting the look of delight in Clay's smiling eyes. He studied her for a moment before saying, "If this is the real Jen, then let's have more, please."

"Oh, I literally jumped out of bed," she said, realizing she'd forgotten to put on her make-up.

Clay reached over and tucked her damp hair behind one ear, unveiling more of her face with its high cheekbones and olive skin.

"You're a natural beauty, do you know that?" he observed, smiling tenderly.

Preoccupied with how to make up for her lack of dinner preparations, Jennie didn't respond to his compliment, although it did not go unnoticed.

Clay asked how her day went and, after listening, Clay smiled affectionately. "No wonder you fell asleep, Jen. That's your body signalling you to stop and smell the roses."

Seizing the moment, Clay dashed off the veranda and raced

to the greenhouse. Finding a rose in bloom, which was mercifully thornless, he twisted this way and that, but the tough, now stringy piece of lengthy stem remained attached. He reached into his pocket and withdrew a jackknife to finish the job.

"Not exactly the gallant move I imagined," he laughed, "but here, inhale the sensuous aroma of this beauty," he said, holding the champagne-coloured blossom under Jennie's nose.

She inhaled the scent slowly, enjoying Clay's bit of theatre. Setting the flower aside, she rose on her tiptoes and planted a quick kiss on his cheek.

"That really is the most perfect rose, Clay." She smiled before inhaling the scent a second time. "Mmm, so sensual," she murmured, surprised by her choice of words.

Still holding the stem, she settled into the soft green cushions of the settee, fixing her gaze on Clay.

"Look, Jen," he said, gently. "How about you pour yourself a glass of something good, and I'll buzz over to the village and bring us one of those wood-fired pizzas from Antonio's? Would you like that?"

"You're a gift from the gods," Jennie replied. "And after supper, I'll let you know why I don't think I can do this anymore."

Clay's downcast gaze suggested to Jennie that Clay thought she was referring to their relationship. She stood up and rushed toward him, placing one hand on his shoulder in a reassuring gesture.

"Oh, gosh no, Clay, I wasn't talking about us." She squeezed the skin between his neck and shoulders as if giving him a quick hug. And then, glancing down at the ground before meeting Clay's gaze, she said, "I mean this business."

Wrapping his arms around Jennie, Clay whispered in her

left ear, "Aw, Jen, I can see you've hit rock bottom. I could see it coming." He pulled her in closer, and Jennie instinctively returned the embrace, her eyes tearing up.

Releasing his embrace, Clay continued. "Now, promise me you'll relax here for a bit. Get yourself that drink, and I'll be back before you know it… just don't fall asleep if you can help it," he said, chuckling.

"And after dinner, I'm looking forward to looking at your business model and seeing if we can help make things more manageable for you."

Clay's words felt like a lifeline thrown Jennie's way. After Derrick's passing, she finally got used to using singular pronouns in this new phase of her life. But she sorely missed the collegial spirit implied by the word *we*.

"Business model," Jennie repeated in a small voice. "I guess that'd be the fly-by-the-seat-of-your-pants business model," she laughed softly, surrendering any semblance of being in command of her own business.

By the time Clay returned with a large fungi pizza, Jennie already felt a relaxed buzz after her gin and tonic. She had resisted the urge to change her clothes and apply some makeup. Instead, she grabbed a plush throw from the living room sofa and settled on the veranda to enjoy her drink.

Café dinner jazz played through the speakers on the veranda as they ate their supper. Jennie became increasingly mellow. She turned to Clay after they'd finished eating and remarked, "You know, the best times happen when they're not planned, don't you think?"

"I agree," said Clay, gathering up dishes and the remains of their impromptu supper. When he returned from the kitchen, he asked to see Jennie's accounting records.

❧

J ENNIE FELT ready to admit defeat but allowed herself a moment before opening her books to him. She imagined it would be like letting Clay see her naked body for the first time.

Her mind flashed back to her childhood when she was ten years old. A friend's brother had discovered her diary while snooping under her bed. He read it aloud in front of his sister, exposing secrets about her. Mortified, Jennie not only lost a close friend that day, but also endured jeers on the playground, in the school hallway, and in the washroom.

Clay detected her reticence. "If you want me to offer some advice," he said gently, "then I need to know the numbers, and I need to know the routines. So, I'm asking you to trust a man who's been in business for over 25 years."

"In the paragliding business, you mean, Clay?"

"No, the hotel business," he said, much to Jennie's surprise. "I bought a boutique hotel in Dublin way back when, and I still have a share in it," he said proudly.

"But when my wife and I split, I no longer wanted to live in Ireland, and I couldn't see running a business across oceans."

"Whoa, that's a lot of information to absorb suddenly," Jennie exclaimed.

"Yes, I'm sure," replied Clay, understandingly. "But I wanted you to know a bit about my background, especially when we have a few things in common."

Jennie wondered if these commonalities had something to do with their mutual attraction. Clay's statement threw Jennie into deep thought.

We have similarities but our lifestyle choices are so different that I can't envision a serious relationship forming. Clay is also vastly different from Derrick. I struggle to imagine a future with him.

Derrick was meticulous about his work. He didn't take short-cuts; for instance, he wouldn't just paint over an old dresser. He'd strip it and refinish it to 'new' condition. Clay, on the other hand, seems like the type who wouldn't even bother with owning a dresser if he had the choice.

Derrick rarely missed a day of work, and those days often extended into weekends. In some ways, he seemed to dedicate his life to providing for his family, always emphasizing the importance of saving for a 'rainy day'.

Bringing Jennie back into the conversation, Clay continued. "I've experienced both highs and lows, as most business owners do, but I'm happy to say that I'm doing very well financially," Clay elaborated.

Then he added, "And I'm sure you can see I enjoy my life. I just want the same for you, Jen," he said, his expression sincere.

They settled into the home office, and Clay examined Jennie's accounting records. It didn't take him long to see where he could make suggestions to help her streamline her business or close it down and start over.

At first, she became defensive when he asked questions such as, "Do you buy your supplies wholesale? Do you use the most inexpensive ingredients you can find to make your lavish breakfasts? Do you hire housekeepers?"

Clay quickly understood that Jennie was proud of the family tradition of not hiring outside help unless necessary. And to strive for 'perfection' in everything she did.

"Yes, you can keep doing what you have been doing, and it looks like you pay your son's tuition expenses and installment payments on that debt load you're carrying, barely, but I think it's time to consider your options."

Jennie listened attentively, considering all of Clay's suggestions. It felt good to share her mounting concerns with someone who seemed to care. With Clay, she soon overcame her fear of revealing her accounting information.

Jennie ceased being defensive when she realized Clay wasn't there to pass judgment but genuinely wanted to help.

"Yes, I make muffins and all the apple pancakes from scratch. I provide hormone-free, local bacon. I offer the best coffee I can find and serve it in pottery mugs I crafted myself. Mom picks fresh flowers from our garden and arranges them in vases. I also showcase my pottery for sale."

"No wonder your guests love it here," Clay said. "Yours is the jewel in the crown of local B&Bs, no doubt." He paused for a moment before adding, "In fact, your reputation for excellence has spread far and wide, I suspect, judging by the license plates I see on vehicles parked in your driveway."

Clay looked straight into Jennie's eyes. Stroking her cheek, he asked tenderly, "But what's all that perfection doing to you, Jen? Is it worth it to chase money and not live your life to the fullest?"

Jennie felt the truth of his words. They stayed up well after midnight, discussing ideas and options. Jennie tried to be objective, viewing things with a business mindset. She grappled with the choice of continuing things as they were, and making changes that might allow her to run a profitable business, while having the freedom to do the things she loved.

In the end, Jennie agreed to hire help to do the changeovers. No more would she do the guest laundry or housecleaning of the rooms. In the breakfast room, she would serve French toast instead of apple pancakes and offer a bowl of hard-boiled eggs for those who wanted them. Easy clean-up. Fewer choices.

No, she wouldn't compromise on the coffee, even if it kept guests lingering longer than optimal in the breakfast room. But she would offer one-litre bags of local coffee for sale, besides her stock of homemade pottery.

"How can I afford to hire help when I can barely make ends meet as is?" she asked Clay.

"You'll reduce expenditures by making the changes we discussed. You'll earn at least some income from selling coffee and pottery."

Clay offered more suggestions. "I'll build a roadside farm stand so you can sell produce such as strawberries, corn, herbs, flowers, eggs… whatever you want. It all adds up."

"You can trade hay bales," he continued, " for having your hay cut and baled." Clay didn't stop at that. "Or, you could consider buying a flock of sheep and letting them mow your fields."

An idea that intrigued Jennie was Clay's suggestion that she could rent campsites on part of her property.

Hearing Clay's confident delivery lifted Jennie's spirits. She realized she wasn't stuck after all. She had options.

"But, if I were you, Jennie, I'd scrap the whole B&B idea and find a way that is far easier to manage, a way that doesn't make you feel like you're on call 24/7, and a way that decreases your risk of housing questionable guests."

In his way of making things seem more manageable, Clay said, "But let's just start with the few ideas we've discussed, and we can consider bigger changes later."

Jennie smiled with gratitude, hopeful of a brighter future to come. But her energy was drained after the long day. She attempted to stifle her yawn, but couldn't manage it.

Clay allowed his yawn to escape freely, his mouth stretching wide, revealing the glint of his teeth as he stretched his arms overhead, his muscles rippling beneath the fabric of his shirt.

Pushing back his chair from the desk, he retrieved his wallet from a clear spot he had found on the bookshelf.

He and Jennie walked across the living room together and,

once out on the veranda, Clay turned to her and said, "Listen, you have a great sleep, Jen, and I may see you across the fields tomorrow. Other than that, let's get together in a few days. Sound good?"

Jennie enveloped Clay in a warm hug, savouring the embrace for longer than usual, and before releasing entirely, she impulsively reached up and kissed him on the lips.

Driven by a deep sense of gratitude, the gesture seemed natural. More than that, Jennie admitted to herself that her feelings for Clay had reached another level.

Even though she recognized there was no guarantee that the changes would succeed, hearing of possibilities reignited her spirit. She felt proud of her openness to new ideas, and her willingness to try something different.

Before Clay had intervened, all she could sense was a looming disaster, but now there was a glimmer of hope on the horizon. She would take her time to consider the options, but for now, she had to stick with her routines.

Just as Jennie released her quick kiss, Clay gently drew her back in, his lingering kiss infused with warmth and tenderness. When they finally released each other, Jennie was breathless.

"Um, ah," she muttered, smoothing back her hair. She could think of nothing to say other than, "I'll lock the door after you leave, Clay."

"See you soon, Jen." He winked, and as he walked away, she admired his muscular physique for a moment longer before closing the front door and turning the lock against the unknown.

CHAPTER 17

On the following afternoon, enveloped by the promise of spring buds on the verge of blooming, and the ever-changing vista of their waterfront property, Jennie approached her mother with the delicate task of discussing her financial situation, choosing her words with utmost care and gentleness.

She needn't have worried. Kathleen had been around the block a few times, and she rarely heard anything entirely new anymore, or so she claimed.

Kathleen listened without interrupting until Jennie finished her explanation. Then she reached over and rested her left hand on Jennie's right shoulder.

"Yours is a story as old as time, my dear. It may seem to you like it's the end of the world, but believe me, we can and will find our way out of this. It's only a temporary blip in paradise."

Kathleen laughed softly. "We won't let the rotten apples spoil the barrel, if I may use an analogy suitable to our heritage," she said, glancing toward the apple orchard.

A gentle smile broke Jennie's sullen face as she listened to her mother. She felt relieved to have informed Kathleen of what she regarded as a dire situation.

Warmed by the instant support of her cherished mother, Jennie declared, "You make it sound so easy, Mom."

"Oh, I didn't say it would be easy, but I know it's possible," Kathleen declared confidently, lifting her chin as if to dismiss any doubts or contrary notions.

Jennie felt fatigued, even though the day was far from over. She drew Kathleen in close, kissing her on one cheek.

"Thanks, Mom, for your positivity; it means the world to me. And now I need a cup of tea. Shall I make us a fresh pot?"

"Oh, by the way, dear," Kathleen called after Jennie. "Did a nice young fellow by the name of Clay come to see you?"

Jennie chuckled. "Why, yes, Mom. Thanks for sending him my way."

Jennie couldn't help smiling, though she restrained herself from revealing too much to her mother just then. It seemed premature to admit that Clay, in a very short time, had infused her life with a new dimension, sparking excitement and possibilities. And she might even add the word *intrigue*.

"We've worked something out, so don't be surprised if you see him and his students traipsing across the fields with their paragliding equipment."

Kathleen grinned. "Good. He seems like such a nice man. You know, he rents the old Johnson farm on Arbutus Lane. Did he mention that?"

Oddly, Jennie noticed a hint of smugness in Kathleen's demeanour, as if she took pride in knowing something about Clay that Jennie did not. It almost seemed to Jennie as though her mother wanted to claim credit for introducing them.

"No, Mom, he did not mention that. But, honestly, we had so much to talk about..." Jennie's voice trailed off as she revisited scenes from their time together.

Kathleen beamed with pleasure, especially when Jennie recounted their kayaking trip to Hudson Point.

"Don't get any ideas, Mom," Jennie warned playfully. "I'm not looking for a man."

"I know, dear. But it's about time you had some fun, don't you think?"

"I have to admit, it felt good to have an adventure with someone close to my age, regardless of gender. But if you think I'm looking for a serious relationship, I'm not. You know as well as I do, no one could ever replace Derrick."

CHAPTER 18

After the morning paragliding lesson, Clay said goodbye to his two students and, leaving his equipment on the clifftop, walked across the field, past the barn, and headed toward the veranda.

Ascending the three steps, he spotted Kathleen sitting on the green settee with Jennie entering through the front hall carrying two cups of coffee on a tray. With the breakfast room closed for the day, Jennie decided to take a breather before diving into the cleanup.

"Good Morning, Jen; nice to see you taking a break," Clay greeted warmly, a look of delight evident on his face as he observed Jennie giving herself some respite after their previous discussions.

"Feels pretty darn good, Clay," Jennie replied, beaming brightly.

Approaching Kathleen, Clay greeted her in an unconventional manner by pressing his palms together in a prayer-like fashion and bending forward slightly.

"Good morning, Kathleen," he said with a smile.

Jennie's cheeks flushed. She couldn't help but steal a glance at Kathleen, trying to gauge her reaction to what she and her mother had customarily called a 'hippie greeting'. Kathleen, however, didn't show any surprise or discomfort, which Jennie found intriguing.

"It's so nice to see you again," Clay said, his smile radiant as he resumed an upright position.

"Clay," Kathleen said, returning his smile, "it's lovely to see you, too."

As Jennie set the tray on the coffee table and slid it closer to Kathleen, she continued to eavesdrop on their conversation.

"I hope you don't mind us launching from Cliffhouse," Clay said, settling on the edge of a wicker glider.

Kathleen's eyes sparkled with a mysterious glint. Her faint smile hinted at a concealed story waiting to unfold. "Oh," she chuckled softly, "Jennie tells me your arrangement is going quite smoothly."

"It sure is. Thank you, Kathleen," Clay replied gratefully. "We often see your guests watching us launch. I'm hoping it'll become an added feature for your business."

"Yes," Kathleen agreed. "I also see them meandering through the fields toward the clifftop. And they seem to love being on the farm, particularly watching our palomino in the corral, and sometimes exploring the barn. We have a lot to offer here."

"You sure do, and I feel blessed to be here." Clay remarked, his smile widening. "And, in a way, I feel the universe brought us together in this time and space."

Graciously nodding in agreement, Kathleen rose from her chair. "Jen, perhaps Clay would like at cup of coffee. I'm fine with the one I had earlier; don't want to overdo it, if you know what I mean," she chuckled to herself.

Glancing at Clay, she added, "I must feed the chickens now, so I'll leave you two alone."

As Kathleen hastened down the chip trail toward the henhouse, she shouted over her shoulder in her sing-song voice, "Lovely to see you again, Clay!"

"Would you like some coffee, Clay?" Jennie offered, seizing the opportunity to learn more about him.

"I'd love to, Jen. I can spare half an hour or so, then I have to head out," Clay replied, getting up from his chair and heading toward the hallway entrance.

"Oh, let me do it. The breakfast room's a mess," Jennie interjected, a hint of anxiety in her voice.

"Nothing I haven't seen before, I promise you," Clay reassured her, continuing on his way.

Seated back on the veranda, Clay took a sip. "Whoa, that's scorching hot," he exclaimed.

Jennie rushed into the kitchen, returning with a glass of iced water. "Here, that'll help," she offered kindly. "I hate when that happens," she said empathetically. "So sorry, Clay. I guess the coffee overheated after sitting there for so long, I don't know."

"No worries, Jen, but thanks for the water. It helps," Clay replied gratefully.

Jennie settled back into her chair. "Clay, I was thinking about you the other day," she claimed, though in truth, she found it hard to get him off her mind since their last meeting. "I realized I know little about your background, but you mentioned you met Derrick while in Victoria. Are you from B.C. then?"

"Born and raised in Courtenay," he affirmed proudly.

"Nice. Are you a skier?" she asked, recalling the weekends she and Derrick spent skiing Mount Washington.

"Sure, I like to ski sometimes, but paragliding is my favourite sport, as you can imagine," he replied with a chuckle.

"Of course," Jennie replied. "Your passion for the sport is heart-warming." After a brief pause, Jennie launched into the questions she wanted to ask. "Did you remain on Vancouver Island your whole life, then? Did you attend school here, for instance?"

Clay's turquoise eyes beamed with delight, perhaps pleased with Jennie's interest in his background. "Yes, I took some business courses at UVic, which I found useful as I moved on to managing a small hotel in Dublin and then in managing my paragliding business here in B.C."

With raised brows and widened eyes, Jennie was curious. "Dublin? What took you over there?"

"Marriage."

Jennie listened intently, surprised by a puzzling tinge of disappointment rising in her chest.

"Yes, around the time I met Derrick, I also met a woman in a bar in Victoria. She captured my heart and, long story short, I followed her back to Ireland. We got married soon after and had a beautiful baby boy."

Jennie brought her coffee cup to her lips, attempting to hide her jealousy. Choking, she cleared her throat before composing herself. "Uh, I assume you're no longer married?" Holding her breath, Jennie awaited his reply.

Clay's expression softened. "No, Jen. The divorce was finalized two years ago, sadly."

Jennie remained silent, hoping Clay would elaborate. Yet, she didn't want to pry.

"You see, Barbara worked as an RN in Dublin but kindly agreed to give it a go here in B.C. when she realized I wasn't happy living in the city," Clay explained.

Jennie nodded understandingly. "You don't strike me as a city type, Clay."

"No, I'm not. And the hotel business was successful, but she knew I wasn't happy. I mean, I wouldn't have asked her to, but she studied hard and passed the Canadian board exams. With a shortage of nurses in Victoria, she got a job right away. Besides, she wanted to make our marriage work."

"Yeah," Jennie murmured sympathetically. "She must have loved you very much, Clay."

Clay didn't respond right away, so Jennie continued wanting to keep the conversation going. "Barbara sounds like a remarkable woman," Jennie remarked, her voice filled with admiration. "To make such sacrifices for your happiness, that's real love."

Clay nodded, a hint of melancholy in his eyes. "She did, Jen. She did. But sometimes, even love isn't enough to mend what's broken."

Jennie placed a reassuring hand on Clay's arm. "I'm sorry things didn't work out as you hoped, Clay."

Clay offered a small smile. "Thanks, Jen. It's life, right? I know she wanted me to be happy, and she loved what she saw of Vancouver Island on her brief visit so many years before."

"We were both willing to try. Unfortunately, like so many other healthcare workers, she burned out while she was working at the Jubilee Hospital in Victoria."

"Oh, how sad," said Jennie. "Did she go back to Ireland?"

"Yep. She and Patrick moved in with her parents in October 2014. One year later, she asked me for a divorce."

"I'm sorry, Clay," Jennie said empathetically, drawing on her own experience of loss. "You've been through a lot. And what about your son?"

"Patrick returned to Dublin with Barbara. He was 17 years old."

"Is he still there, Clay?"

"Yes. When he graduated from high school, we gifted him a trip to B.C." Clay smiled proudly.

" He visited me while I was still in Victoria, and then again last year after I'd settled here on Sunrise Island. He fell in love with B.C. and talked about moving here. We're not sure what will happen."

The word "we" hung in the air, casting an unwelcome presence over Jennie's thoughts. *Oh, come on,* she told herself. *You also have a history of marriage with children.* Puzzled by her rising feelings of jealousy and concern that Clay would forever be bound to Barbara through their son Patrick, she felt conflicted.

"Look, I have to get on with the clean-up, Clay, but thanks so much for letting me know your story." Gathering the coffee cups and placing them on her tray, she rose from her chair, wished Clay a good afternoon, and left the veranda in a quandary.

On the one hand, Clay's story made it feel like she now had a good reason not to move forward with him. On the other, there were those feelings of jealousy that told her there may be something more between them than she had realized.

CHAPTER 19

The sky had turned cloudy and, by the time the sun sank below the horizon, there were only a few streaks of pink sunset to the west.

Weary at the end of her workday, Jennie stretched out on the chaise longue, while Kathleen enjoyed another cup of jasmine tea, made with the leaves of their own summer jasmine flowers.

The scent of the intensely, sweet-smelling flowers wafted across their seating area. "That scent will forever remind me of home, Mom," Jennie said tenderly.

"Oh, I know. Can't be without my jasmine tea." Waiting for it to cool, Kathleen seemed to have something on her mind. She glanced at Jennie, then turned toward the front yard. "So," she ventured, "What do you think of Clay, dear?"

Jennie chuckled softly. She had anticipated this question. It seemed to her Kathleen hoped they would become a couple, even though she hadn't explicitly expressed such a wish. It was just that gleam in her eye, her apparent delight whenever he visited.

Maybe, thought Jennie, *Mom has noticed my increased energy lately.* Amused at herself folding towels joyfully one day, Jennie couldn't help but notice how the usually tedious chores had somehow become pleasurable. Instead of thinking about how worn the towels were getting, she was thinking about Clay. Endlessly.

"Mom, it's only been a year since we lost Derrick, I know that. And you can't put a timeline on grief."

"Aw, I know that, Jen. No one can replace Derrick; I get that. And Clay is very different from Derrick, don't you think?"

"Very. He hates gardening. He doesn't even want to hear about fertilizing the roses or pruning the hedges. It's just not in his vocabulary," she chuckled.

"Does he play tennis, dear?" Kathleen seemed hopeful.

"Nope. He doesn't ride either. But he skis, I found out today. His passion, as we both know, is paragliding."

"He takes care of his health, it looks like, and that's so important, isn't it Jen?"

Jennie laughed inwardly, sensing her mother's subtle attempts to highlight Clay's positive qualities. "Yes, I believe so, Mom, but that hippie thing he does…"

"What's the harm, Jennie? It seems rather gracious, I'd say, and remember that your own daughter Kyla lives in a commune."

"How could I forget, Mom?" They shared a laugh and Jennie added, "And how many times does Kyla talk about 'the universe'?"

"Oh, I know, Jen, but again, what's the harm?"

"True, Mom. Clay and Kyla share a few quirks, but they're both good-hearted and well-intentioned… at least we know Kyla is," she added with amusement.

"And I can see that Clay is fun-loving. He's full of energy like Derrick was, although Clay shows it with a slower step,"

Kathleen remarked with a hint of delight. She paused for a moment before continuing. "Remember how you couldn't see a way forward after Derrick passed?"

"I sure do. I truly didn't think I could make it; yet, I knew I must. I just didn't know how," Jennie recalled with a somber tone.

"Not only did you move forward without Derrick, but you became a successful business owner, managing the demands of the B&B and earning enough profit to handle the property and other expenses. Jennie, I knew you could do it, Kathleen praised warmly."

"Aw, thanks, Mom. It feels good, but I'm not in any hurry to have a serious relationship. I still miss Derrick terribly, so how can I even think about getting permanently involved with someone else?"

CHAPTER 20

"Oh, this is just lovely," exclaimed a woman with curly hair, about Jennie's age, as she swung open her car door, about to check in to Room Three. Jennie had observed her arrival, noting how considerately she had parked in the turn-around to allow space for other vehicles to get by.

"Well, hello," greeted Ingrid warmly, extending her hand adorned with silver bangles. "You must be Jennie Mitchell.

As they shook hands, Jennie replied, "And you must be Ingrid. Welcome to Cliffhouse by the Sea."

"Why, thank you. I already adore it here. You know, you and I have something in common," Ingrid remarked with a warm smile.

Intrigued, Jennie tilted her head slightly and asked, "Oh, what's that?"

"We're both widows," Ingrid revealed, her smile softening.

Surprised, Jennie's eyebrows rose as she asked, "How did you know that?"

Ingrid chuckled. "It's that small-town vibe, I suppose. While chatting with the server in the café at Fulford Harbour, she asked where I was headed. When I mentioned Cliffhouse by the Sea, I got the whole lowdown, including that detail about you."

Although somewhat taken aback by the local's candidness, Jennie chose to view it in a positive light. "Well," she responded, raising her chin slightly in confidence, "that's what you want when you run a business. Positive chatter. I assume she spoke favourably?"

Ingrid nodded reassuringly, her smile widening. "Absolutely. She even mentioned that yours was the top B&B on the island"

Delighted, Jennie responded graciously, her eyes brightening with genuine interest."You know, there are some fantastic B&Bs here on Sunrise. Sometimes you have to book a year in advance to get your preferred spot."

Wanting to deepen the connection with Ingrid, Jennie returned to their shared experience, her tone gentle and empathetic. "When did you become a widow, Ingrid?"

Ingrid's expression softened, a wistful smile playing gently on her lips. "I lost my William three years ago today. That's why I'm taking some time to myself. Sort of a celebration of our lives together."

Instantly, Jennie sensed an unspoken understanding pass between them, a silent acknowledgment of shared pain and resilience.

Moved by Ingrid's openness, a profound empathy moved Jennie to share her own story. "I lost Derrick just over a year ago," she began, sharing the details of her own journey.

With no plans for dinner other than leftovers from the fridge, Jennie extended an invitation. "Ingrid, if you're interested, perhaps we could head into town for a meal after you get settled in. Of course, if you have other plans..."

Before Jennie could finish, Ingrid eagerly interjected. "I'd love that, Jennie. I'm not sure if you enjoy seafood, but coming from Calgary, fresh seafood is a real treat for me. I was hoping to try some local fish."

"I love seafood, and I know just the place," Jennie assured her.

"Only if it's caught fresh," she insisted. "No farmed seafood for me."

"This is Sunrise Island, my dear," Jennie declared proudly. "We only serve the freshest catches."

"Perfect," smiled Ingrid. "Does 6:30 work for you?"

"Yes, I'll make a reservation, and I'll drive so you can enjoy the scenery, if that's okay."

"Absolutely," Ingrid nodded appreciatively. "I'll be ready."

Conversation flowed effortlessly as they drove to the restaurant called Seaglass, renowned for its fresh-caught crab and halibut fish and chips. Jennie felt as if they'd been friends forever, wishing that Ingrid lived closer than Calgary.

"So, have you dated since Derrick's passing, if you don't mind my asking?" ventured Ingrid.

Jennie chuckled. "Well, there's a guy who seems interested in me, but you know how it goes..."

"I remember those feelings well. When I first dated someone, about a year and a half after William passed, it was a mix of excitement and uncertainty," shared Ingrid.

"I wanted to make a connection, but felt like a teenager again," Jennie admitted, "somehow new at the game."

"So, you were ready to start a new relationship," Jennie remarked, curious about Ingrid's experience.

"Yes, absolutely. I've never been good at being alone," confessed Ingrid.

Jennie contemplated her situation. "I keep myself busy most of the time. It's like I barely have time to realize I'm alone," she chuckled. "Truth be told, after my workday is done, I sometimes crave solitude."

"Yes, I can see how that might play out for you, Jennie. But my therapist might say you avoid your pain by keeping busy," suggested Ingrid gently.

Jennie nodded. "Perhaps. But I think about Derrick all the time. It's hard not to, especially when I see reminders of him everywhere."

"I know what you mean, Jennie. It was the same for me, although the images occur less frequently now. Tell me, what kinds of images do you see?"

"I see him in the yard, pruning the roses, feeding our horse, sitting beside me upstairs in the bedroom we shared."

"Uh huh," Ingrid smiled, "and I bet you sometimes talk to him as though he was still in the room."

"I do," said Jennie, "less than before though. Sleeping alone in bed was one of the hardest adjustments.

"I know what you mean. It took time, but eventually, I got used to it," shared Ingrid.

Jennie paused, her fork-load of halibut hovering. "You mean you got used to not having William beside you?"

Ingrid shook her head. "No, he's always with me. But I accepted his absence and moved forward. It takes time, though."

"I'm struggling with that. I'm afraid it will affect any new relationship," confided Jennie.

Ingrid reached across the table, squeezing Jennie's hand. "Don't be afraid. Embrace life as it comes. Life goes on if we let it."

Jennie felt a wave of warmth at Ingrid's words, as though

she had received the gift of wisdom. "Thank you, Ingrid. Your words mean a lot."

"What's your new relationship like, if you don't mind me asking?" Jennie inquired.

"You can ask me anything, Jennie," Ingrid reassured, taking a sip of her chardonnay.

"You know, I'd say it's everything you might hope it would be. We share everything—from mundane tasks to planning trips. We share coffee in bed on weekends and cook together during the week."

"I don't mean to paint a picture of perfection," she cautioned, "that doesn't exist. But we've learned to embrace forgiveness and cherish each other every day." As Ingrid spoke, her expression radiated contentment.

Jennie's mind drifted to the possibility of having a tennis partner again, someone to share the simple joys of everyday life. She envisioned moments filled with laughter with someone who enjoyed her company as much as she enjoyed his. A glimmer of anticipation shone brightly in Jennie's eyes.

"To new beginnings," toasted Jennie, raising her glass. "Thank you for sharing your story with me, Ingrid. Maybe the universe is showing me a way forward."

Ingrid smiled back. "Here's to second chances, Jennie. I believe you'll find yours when the time is right."

CHAPTER 21

As time flowed by, memories of Derrick gradually receded in Jennie's mind, making way for vivid images of her and Clay.

An idyllic afternoon at Honeymoon Cove lingered in her thoughts. They had stood barefoot on smooth stones warmed by the sun, making Jennie wonder why she'd ever want to do anything else. The gentle breeze carried the scent of saltwater and seaweed, while the sound of seagulls filled the air, adding to the serenity of the moment.

Memories of an enchanting summer evening when they kayaked in the ocean remained etched in Jennie's mind. As they dipped their kayak paddles into the water, a mesmerizing display unfolded—silver and neon blue swirls created by bioluminescent algae rewarded their senses with a magical spectacle. Each stroke of the paddle seemed to ignite the water, leaving a trail of shimmering light in its wake. In those moments, surrounded by luminescent beauty, Jennie felt a profound connection to Clay and the world around her.

Clay had peeled back Jennie's veil of grief, revealing the playful, vibrant woman he suspected lay beneath all along.

THEY WAITED until Monday to escape to Driftwood Beach at the far southern tip of the island. Jennie mentioned that the B&B would be less bustling that day, and Clay noted that the popular spots were usually less crowded.

As they perched side-by-side on a huge driftwood log, Jennie gazed out at the swirling expanse of the ocean, feeling as though she were Alice caught in a dizzying whirl, on the brink of tumbling into another realm.

High-pitched trills of oystercatchers, with their vibrant orange bills and pink legs, pierced the air while birds on the rocks staked their territorial boundaries.

A mammoth driftwood tree trunk lay sprawled across the stony beach, towering over the surrounding logs, and inviting the adventurous to test their balance by walking along its uneven, asymmetrical surface.

"What if we were to sing everything, not speak our words?" asked Clay, breaking the serene atmosphere.

"What if we were to sing everything, not speak our words?" Jennie playfully echoed. Clay chuckled, initially unaware that Jennie was engaging in an old game of annoying repetition.

"Words our speak not…" Clay laughed. "Speaking backward requires a special talent. It's not just repeating what someone else says," he replied, catching on to Jennie's playful mood.

Their laughter resonated through the salty breeze, infusing Jennie with a sense of childlike delight. As they wandered along the shoreline, they stumbled upon a low promontory extending toward the sea.

"This is the best spot on the entire beach," Clay proclaimed as they settled into another nook.

"It feels like we're perched on the bow of a ship," observed Jennie, revelling in the expansive vistas of the ocean.

As a barge loaded with colossal shipping containers passed by, Jennie's curiosity piqued.

"I suppose that cargo ship is off to faraway ports—or maybe just Vancouver," she chuckled. "What do you think are in those containers, Clay?"

"Consumer products, the bane of the world," said Clay, injecting a bit of humour into his response.

"Alright, alright," said Jennie, "I see where this is headed."

"What do you mean?" Clay inquired, his expression growing more serious.

Jennie hesitated for a moment, sensing the weight of their interaction. She chose her words carefully, mindful of the potential impact on their relationship.

"My daughter Kyla, who calls herself Sundance, is a naturalist like you. Her go-to topics of conversation revolve around organic gardening, consumer waste, and saving old-growth forests."

"And you have a problem with that?" Clay's gaze held a hint of concern.

Jennie took a moment to consider her response, knowing that Clay was usually non-judgemental. "Not at all. But I admit I often go the convenience route when I just don't have time to do the right thing, you might say," she chuckled. "But I refuse to feel guilty about it."

"Fair enough," Clay responded. "We do what we can, right?" He put his right arm across her shoulders, gently pulled her in close, and then released her. Jennie admired Clay's acceptance and wished she could embody more of that attitude herself.

They watched a gleaming white cruise ship pass by, speculating it was on its way to Alaska. "Queen of the Sea, all dressed up for an all-white tea," mused Jennie, delighted with her impromptu rhyme.

A few sailboats anchored nearby, one with red-and-white striped sails catching Jennie's eye. "I think I'll name that one Peppermint Stick," she said. "It's off to Secret Island, no doubt."

"More like the S.S. Money-sucker," laughed Clay. "I used to own a sailboat. I traded sailing on the sea for sailing in the sky, and it's a lot more affordable."

They strolled across the surface of the sandstone shelf, carefully examining the intricate tide pools. Jennie spotted a slime-covered dime at the bottom of one pool amidst the barnacles and lipids.

Without hesitation, she squatted down and reached her bare hand into the pool, attempting to retrieve the pseudo treasure.

"Fish for a dime covered with slime," quipped Clay.

They carried on this way for much of the afternoon, feeling comfortable enough in each other's company to let their inner child come out to play.

As DUSK SETTLED, they decided it was time to head back. Walking through a forest of Douglas fir trees toward the parking lot. Jennie took the lead but paused halfway, turning to face Clay.

"I'm not entirely sure where the trail is," she admitted with a shrug.

"Then make your own trail. That way, you can't get lost,"

Clay suggested, his words holding more personal significance to Jennie than he likely intended.

Before Jennie could turn around and try a different route, Clay leaned in for a kiss. Jennie's response was instinctive.

She reached out, placed her hands on the back of his neck, and swept them up into his wind-tossed hair as if it was the most natural thing in the world for her to do. As their kiss deepened, she felt herself melting into his embrace, enveloped in a sense of safety and love.

The forest, her sanctuary, seemed to echo the peace she felt in that moment.

But when Clay whispered in her ear, "Can we spend the night together sometime soon?" Jennie froze.

She knew she wasn't ready for the next level, yet she sensed Clay's patience wearing thin, despite his efforts to hide it.

Planting a quick kiss on his lips, Jennie slid her hands down his bare arms and grasped both of his hands. "I'd love that, Clay, but please understand that I need more time."

"How much more time do you need, Jen?" Clay asked patiently. "We met in early April when I came begging to rent a launch site at Cliffhouse. That was three months ago."

Jennie released his hands, struck by the imploring look in Clay's eyes. "You know how you suggested I make my own trail?"

Clay nodded, apparently waiting for her explanation.

"Clay," Jennie began, her voice soft yet resolute. "I need to listen to my heart, and I know you'll understand that," Jennie began. "When we take our relationship to the next level, I want to do it with my entire spirit on board. I'm almost there, Clay, but something is holding me back."

Clay gazed out into the forest before responding, "I know

you still think about Derrick, Jen." He paused, his hand gently touching his heart as if to symbolize the depth of her feelings.

Clay fixed his gaze on Jennie's soft brown eyes. "That's only natural. We honour our loved ones by remembering them. But if your remembrance is so strong that it prevents you from moving ahead," he continued, his tone gentle yet firm, "then how can you open your heart to new love?"

Clay's gentle yet passionate plea echoed in Jennie's heart, urging her to release herself from the invisible ties that held her back. She couldn't deny it. Yet, in the depths of her being... she believed she wasn't ready to break free and step into a new chapter.

"I'm sure you're right, Clay; in fact, I know you're right. Please believe me when I say I'm so close. I want it to happen, and you'll know when I'm ready," Jennie reassured him with a smile, but Clay wore a solemn expression.

"Yes, of course, Jen. Just so you know... I envision us walking hand-in-hand. It's not my style to push anyone into a relationship. What I want is not just physical intimacy; I want to share a deeper connection with you."

Jennie's heart melted at his words, and Clay could probably sense it.

"So, I'll be here, patiently waiting for the moment you feel ready to share your heart with me," he continued softly, brushing her lips with a tender kiss. "But please, don't keep me waiting too long. The thought of what we could have together... it's too precious to wait indefinitely."

"DO YOU SURF, JEN?" Clay asked, just as Jennie opened the passenger door of his SUV, preparing to head into her house.

"Oh," she laughed, "years ago. Derrick and I used to go to Jordan River often in the summer. Why?"

Clay's eyes sparkled with enthusiasm. "Because I was thinking of booking a weekend in a hotel in Tofino. Thought we could surf the waves, feast on some crab, and spend some quality, uninterrupted time together."

Clay had been unusually quiet on the drive back from Driftwood Beach, which left Jennie wondering about his preoccupation. The sudden invitation to Tofino made her feel somewhat uneasy.

Is he trying to establish a timeline for intimacy? Jennie pondered. This side of Clay was unfamiliar to her. Until now, she knew him as someone diligent about work commitments, but more spontaneous in other aspects of his life. And it didn't quite align with their earlier conversation.

"I love Tofino, Clay. Yes, let's plan a weekend away in the future." Jennie smiled sweetly at him as she opened the rear door, gathering her things from the back seat. "The B&B doesn't run itself, though," she said between the seats, "so I'll have to figure out how I can manage it. I'll let you know."

"Don't keep it too long, Jen. They book up quickly. Can you let me know in a couple of days? I was thinking of some time during the last week in June, if you can get help with the B&B."

"I'll let you know on Monday," she said agreeably. As Jennie shut the rear door and waved goodbye to Clay as he circled the drive and headed out, a subtle unease settled in her chest. Despite her outward agreeability, something deep inside of her bristled at the hint of pushiness in Clay's request. While he often offered constructive suggestions to improve the way she managed her business, not once had she felt he was pushing his own agenda until now.

"Thanks for a wonderful day, " Jennie murmured to herself, though her mind raced with conflicting thoughts. Clay's words echoed in her ears, stirring up a whirlwind of uncertainty. *Perhaps I'm being overly cautious*, Jennie thought, but her gut feeling persisted.

It's not unreasonable for a man to want intimacy after a few months, I suppose, she reasoned out loud, trying to rationalize her discomfort. Yet, deep down, Jennie couldn't shake the feeling that something about Clay's sudden urgency didn't sit right with her.

Once inside the house, she busied herself with the task of clearing out Derrick's old clothing. With each piece she folded and placed in the donation box, she couldn't help but reflect on her evolving relationship with Clay and how it contrasted with her memories of Derrick.

CHAPTER 22

Once Clay and Jennie disembarked at the Crofton ferry terminal, they began their journey north toward Tofino. Along the way, they made two stops: one at a service station in Coombs, and another at Cathedral Grove where they took a stroll, immersing themselves in the rich tapestry of scents permeating the forest. The earthy aroma of damp soil mingled with fragrances of cedar and moss and the mild spicy-sweet undertone of the old-growth trees.

Jennie felt her tension melt away in the symphony of woodland perfumes and through the winding roads past peaceful west-coast vistas. Six hours later, they arrived at the resort on Chesterman Beach.

Jennie felt the weight of exhaustion bearing down on her, manifested in the persistent migraines now plaguing her. She interpreted them as a warning sign of overexertion, a signal from her body demanding rest.

In addition to her health concerns, a recent incident served as a wake-up call, highlighting just how thinly she had been spreading herself. It was a clear sign that she needed to step back and reassess her priorities.

While rifling through her kitchen cupboard, she stumbled upon a random teacup adorned with a design of a bird perched on a tree branch. Yet, to her dismay, the bird's tail didn't align with the rest of its body. The incongruity in the cup's design disturbed her deeply, prompting thoughts of donating or repurposed it.

As Jennie chuckled at her tendency toward perfectionism, she realized the deeper truth behind her need for a break. *I need a vacation from myself,* she affirmed, acknowledging the relentless pressure she placed on herself every day.

WHEN THEY CHECKED in at the seaside hotel, a complimentary bottle of champagne awaited them. Clay had mentioned to the Reception, when making the booking, that he and Jennie were celebrating a special occasion.

In their second-floor room, a breath-taking view greeted them: the long sandy beach stretching out to meet the open Pacific Ocean. Without hesitation, they abandoned their plans and rushed out into the surf.

The weather was perfect, and they laughed and played in the waves until Jennie felt thoroughly exhausted. Their rumbling stomachs signalled it was time to rinse off the salt-water and prepare for their 7:00 p.m. dinner reservation.

IN THE SOFT candlelit ambiance of the restaurant overlooking the ocean, they revelled not only in each other's company but also in the sumptuous feast presented by the attentive wait staff. Clay selected a wine suggested by their server to complement the buttered lobster claws. Every bite felt like a taste of heaven to Jennie.

～

As DELIGHTFUL AS the entire day had been, Jennie could barely keep her eyes open. On the way up to their room in the elevator, she called home to check on the family.

When they settled into their luxurious king-sized room, Clay chose the music of the Miles Davis Quintet to round out the night.

Jennie had imagined the two of them slow-dancing as a prelude to the rest of the evening. But when Clay returned from the bathroom, Jennie was fast asleep on the bed, having succumbed to the mellow beats of "You're My Everything", only the second song on the album.

～

WHEN JENNIE's phone chimed loudly at the untimely hour of 6:15 a.m., she and Clay both groaned out loud. Jennie didn't open her eyes.

Clay reached across her recumbent body, retrieved her cell phone from the top of the bedside table, and held it to her ear.

Jennie recognized Alexa's voice at her first word. "Mom, please don't worry, but I wanted to let you know that Grandma fell and might have broken her hip. We don't know."

Jennie gasped, her entire body rigid as she tried to absorb the news.

Alexa's voice carried a hint of hope amidst the shock. "I called 9-1-1, and the ambulance was here in minutes. She's at the Lady Minto Hospital now, Mom. She's in expert hands."

"What happened?" asked Jennie, struggling to remain calm.

"She stood on a step stool trying to reach the top shelf of the kitchen cupboard but must have slipped. Unfortunately, I was doing a changeover, so wasn't in the house. Luckily, Sandy, the guest in Room 1 heard her cry, and rushed to the kitchen."

"Grandma was still conscious when Sandy arrived, she said, but not very lucid.," Alexa reported. "

"That would've been such a shock for you, Lexi," Jennie empathized. "Thank goodness you were there. Thanks for taking time off to fill in for me at the B&B and take care of Mom," Jennie added gratefully. "Oh, please let Sandy know that her stay is complementary."

"I will, Mom, and I've called Kyla to take my place. She's always happy to be away from her job with Dr. Nicholls."

"Okay, thanks. I knew I could rely on my favourite twins. We'll leave here in about fifteen minutes, Lex. Or less," Jennie said before disconnecting the call.

As Jennie prepared to depart, she noticed Clay standing on the balcony, gazing out toward the sea. Feeling guilty for cutting their trip short, she apologized to him while letting him know they'd have to leave right away.

"Let's hope Kathleen hasn't broken her hip," Clay said, his voice full of concern. Understanding the urgency of the situation, Clay offered to bring coffee and the takeout cups provided in the room. "We can grab some takeout on the way."

As THEY SETTLED into the SUV and began the journey home, Jennie immediately called the hospital for an update on Kathleen's condition. She was stable, they assured, but Jennie would have to wait for a call from Dr. Warrington for further details.

Clay had made a ferry reservation to ensure they'd get on board in the busy summer season. He seemed subdued on the way home, prompting Jen to ask if he was okay.

"I'm okay, sweetheart," Clay said, the term of endearment rolling off his tongue with such ease it seemed as if he'd been using it for ages, though in reality, it was the first time he'd called her 'sweetheart'.

Jennie noticed but chose not to mention it.

"I know we have to get back, and it's so unfortunate about your mom's fall." Reaching to touch Jennie's knee, he added, "I sure hope she's alright. She's a gem."

Jennie reached out, placing her hand on top of his knee. "I just hope Mom hasn't broken her hip."

After a while, Clay pulled into the service centre to refuel while Jennie went into the food market, returning with breakfast sandwiches and coffee. They ate in the parking lot to minimize distractions while driving.

Taking a bite of his sandwich, Clay remarked goodnaturedly, "We finally get to spend some quality time together, and then this happens. Funny how things turn out, isn't it, Jen?"

"Yes, I know what you mean, Clay, but who can predict these things? I'm just glad Mom is still with us. She's 81 now, you know."

"Your mom is remarkable," Clay commented. "So full of life and energy. I hope to be like that at her age."

"I used to be," Jennie sighed.

"I noticed yesterday at dinner," Clay said. "It was one of the rare times you seemed to be fully present with me."

His words pierced Jennie's heart, but she wasn't ready to engage in that conversation amidst everything else. "Things will change, eventually. I just need more time," she said softly.

Finishing his sandwich, Clay turned up the music before heading south, taking a moment to express his admiration.

"I love how you take care of Kathleen. It makes me appreciate you even more, if that's possible. And here's a little secret," he added with a smile. "Someday, I'd like to be the lucky guy who receives care and attention like you give your mom."

As Clay's words settled in her mind, Jennie couldn't help but feel uneasy. She wondered if his sentiment was merely a genuine longing for her affection, or was it tinged with self-serving desires? She didn't see Clay as being selfish, she reasoned.

Amidst everything else happening, Jennie wasn't ready to delve into those thoughts any deeper just yet. *Things will change, eventually. I just need more time,"* she told herself, trying to navigate so many emotions.

WHEN THEY FINALLY ARRIVED HOME, they both stepped out of the SUV. Jennie retrieved her luggage from the back seat and joined Clay by the driver's side.

"Are you sure you don't want me to come to the hospital with you, Jen?"

She reached up, cradling her fingers behind his neck. He nestled his hands into the back pockets of her jeans, reminding Jennie of her teenage dating years.

"I'll be fine, Clay, but I appreciate your offering. I'm going to pack a few things Mom might need for her hospital stay and then head out."

"Thank you for a fabulous time, Clay. I loved everything about it except falling asleep before I meant to. I'm so sorry."

"Jen, if you were so relaxed that you fell asleep despite yourself, then the trip was well worth it. Relaxation is the keynote, and we have a lot to look forward to," he said graciously.

They shared a quick kiss, and then Jennie walked toward the kitchen door, as Clay shouted after her. "Let's arrange another overnight as soon as Kathleen is in the clear."

Even though Jennie acknowledged his remark with a smile and a wave, she felt perturbed. *Maybe I'm overreacting, but the last thing I need right now is to be pushed. It's not like Clay to try to steamroll me.*

No matter how things developed, she knew her mother's care would take priority over everything else.

AFTER ARRIVING at the hospital in the late afternoon, Jennie received a report from Dr. Warrington about Kathleen's condition.

"Kathleen did not fracture her hip, fortunately. She has extensive bruising and a hairline fracture in her right wrist."

Jennie nodded, relieved that Kathleen's hip was intact. "I'll take a fractured wrist any day over a broken hip," she remarked to the doctor.

"I should mention that her blood pressure is below normal, Dr Warrington added. "Does she sometimes experience dizziness or lose her balance?"

Jenny thought for a moment. "She hasn't complained about that," she replied. "Do you think she fell off the stool because of dizziness?"

"It's quite possible, given Kathleen's age," Dr. Warrington

nodded. "Might be something to keep an eye on," she added with a smile. "Our physiotherapist, Karen, can give you some exercises that can help improve balance."

Jennie and Kyla helped Kathleen settle back home at Cliffhouse after her extended stay at the hospital. At 81, Kathleen appeared frail, more than a year ago, Jennie noted. With the possibility of balance issues looming, Jennie pondered how to minimize Kathleen's risk of injury.

"It sure makes you take stock of your life when something like this happens, dear," commented Kathleen from the comfort of the veranda. Wrapped in a wool blanket to ward off the morning chill, Kathleen's pleasure at returning home was palpable.

"And, you know, it makes you want to ensure everything is settled before you leave for good," Kathleen added cryptically.

"Mom, let me get you some tea, shall I?" Jennie asked warmly, still enjoying that Kathleen was safe at home.

"Tea?" repeated Kathleen. "I'm in the mood for celebrating, if you don't mind. Would you join me in a glass of bubbly?"

Jennie chuckled, glad to see that Kathleen hadn't lost her spunk, yet was well aware that alcohol, medications, and balance concerns weren't a good mix.

"I sure would, Mom. I have a chilled bottle of sparkling strawberry juice. How does that sound?"

"Sounds bubbly enough for me," Kathleen said, smiling.

"Kyla, what about you?" Jennie asked her daughter.

"Ah, sure. Just enough for a toast, please. I have to get back to the clinic. Dr. Nicholls gets antsy if I'm away too long." Kyla enjoyed her job as a receptionist in the local veterinary clinic, but she found Dr. Nicholls a bit much sometimes.

As soon as Jennie left the room in search of sparkling juice, Kyla leaned in with what appeared to be a burning question. "Grandma, what did you mean about settling things before you pass on?"

Kyla took a moment before adding, "And, just so you know, my dearest grandmother, I never want you to leave us," she affirmed, tilting her head slightly to the right.

Kathleen chuckled good-naturedly. "I know, dear, but we all go someday, even you," she said with a smile before continuing. "I'll give it to you straight, honey, just as I always have."

"Before I die, I'd like to see your mother married, or at least in a serious relationship with Clay."

"Ah," said Kyla, raising her chin and brows at the same time. Kathleen's wish was hardly surprising to anyone, especially Jennie.

"And one more thing. I want to see Jennie have a stable financial future," Kathleen added.

Kyla's face lit up with excitement. "Grandma, Mom paid off her debt months ago, and her business has been turning a profit for more than a year now, I'm pretty sure."

Kathleen's smile appeared even more radiant in the morning light, accentuating her laugh lines, an endearing trait that her family associated with her enjoyment of life.

"Kyla, you've made my day. Now, I have only one more wish to be fulfilled." Kathleen's eyes glistened as Jennie swung open the door carrying three glasses of sparkling juice.

"To Mom," Jennie smiled lovingly, raising her glass. Kathleen and Kyla joined in the cheer while Kathleen piped in. "Jennie, my dear, here's to a bright future for all of us." She winked at Kyla, who smiled knowingly.

CHAPTER 23

*J*enny didn't hear from Clay for the next two weeks. They exchanged waves if they caught sight of each other in the mornings, he on his way to the launch site, she on her way to do the changeovers. One morning, she spotted him taking a tandem flight, something he rarely did, he'd told her. Yet, Jennie was extra busy these days, hardly finding time to notice anything else.

THAT EVENING, Jennie couldn't wait to get into bed. As she ascended the long staircase, using the rail for support after an arduous day, something caught her eye. A long, white envelope with 'Jen' written neatly front and centre, lay strategically on her bedspread. She arranged her pillows for a comfortable sit, anticipating something important.

Awkwardly breaking the seal with her finger, she removed a carefully folded piece of paper. Unfolding the paper, she immediately recognized the handwriting from the times Clay had helped her with plans to make the B&B more manageable.

MY DEAREST JEN,

I HOPE you can forgive me for not telling you this in person. I don't do well with drama. And I can't bear to see you cry.

JENNIE PAUSED FOR A MOMENT, sensing the weight of the words to come. She was already on the edge and knew it wouldn't take much to tip the balance. Setting the letter down on the bed, she drank from a glass of stale water on her bedside table. She took a deep breath, picked up the letter, and continued.

IF 'THE THREE WORDS' mean anything now, I've known for a long time that I love you. I hoped you'd feel the same.

But I can't compete with your memory of Derrick, and I can't compete with your exceptional dedication to your work and perceived responsibilities.

It's not my place and it's not my way to judge any of this. I make no judgments at all. But I know myself, and I know that I needed a solid commitment from you for our relationship to move forward.

JENNIE CHOKED when she read the word 'needed' as if their story had ended.

· · ·

HONESTLY, love, as hard as I've tried and as much as I've yearned for it, I think the universe has a different plan for each of us.

Please know you will always be in my heart, and I genuinely wish you every success in what makes you happy.

CLAY

JENNIE'S HANDS trembled as she held the letter, her fingers unable to maintain their grip as Clay's words sank in. With a gasp, she released her hold, allowing the letter to slip from her hands and fall to the floor. She sat in stunned silence, slowly absorbing Clay's message.

Gasping, Jennie felt as if the weight of the world pressed down on her chest, suffocating her with its magnitude. Her mind spun with emotions, unable to find solid ground amidst the swirling chaos of her thoughts.

Rocking back and forth on the bed, she sought solace in the rhythmic motion, a feeble attempt to steady herself against the onslaught of despair. But there was no escaping the crushing reality of Clay's words, each syllable a painful reminder of the shattered dreams and unfulfilled promises they once shared.

Jennie rose from the bed, her movements clumsy and unco-ordinated as she made her way to her ensuite bathroom. Closing the door behind her, she turned the cold water tap on full. As the tears flowed freely down her cheeks, Jennie surren-dered to the overwhelming tide of grief, allowing herself to be consumed by the raw intensity of her emotions.

When her tears subsided, Jennie felt drained. Looking in the mirror at her tear-ravaged face, she barely recognized her reflec-tion. Turning off the tap, she wet a washcloth and draped it over her face. Despite her efforts, the puffiness remained. She then ran cold water into a hand towel, squeezed out the excess water, and pressed it over both eyes until the towel warmed. *That'll have to do.*

Closing her bedroom drapes, Jennie drew back the covers and climbed into bed, fully clothed. Images of her and Clay replayed incessantly in her mind, and fresh tears streamed down her face, dampening the pillow.

"It's all my fault," she whispered aloud, overwhelmed by despair. As darkness settled, Jennie succumbed to exhaustion, slipping into a deep sleep.

THE SHRILL WHISTLE of storm-force winds drowned out the relentless drumming of rain against the windowpanes. The thick burgundy drapes billowed and danced, pushed by the gusts sneaking through the gap beneath the windows. Despite wearing a full set of clothes, including socks, Jennie felt a persistent chill creeping through her body.

She glanced at her phone, resting on the bedside table, realizing that the alarm would sound in just ten minutes. All she wanted was to succumb to her grief, to stay cocooned in bed with the covers pulled high over her head. But reality loomed—she had to force herself to get up and begin the usual preparations. There was no other option.

NAVIGATING THROUGH HER DAILY ROUTINE, Jennie felt as if she were observing herself from a distance. Despite the relentless storm persisting in full force, she was seized by an undeniable urge to escape.

Kathleen's bedroom door was closed, and not wanting to disturb her, Jennie left her a note on the kitchen table.

I'M TAKING *some time to myself, Mom. I may not be home until after dark. Call me or Alexa if you need anything, okay?*

    Love you,

    Jen

SHE PULLED on her longest raincoat, zipped it up, and tightened the hood. With keys in hand, she hurried to the kitchen, grabbed a tray of frozen carrot and pineapple muffins, and carried it to the breakfast room for the next day. Jennie stepped outside, battling gusts of wind that threatened to slam the outside doors on her fingers.

Opening and closing her car door presented a challenge against the storm but, once inside, she headed down the driveway without her driver's license and any money.

Trying to figure out her destination taxed Jennie's weary brain to the limit. She drove blindly through the stormy weather for half an hour before remembering a spot where she might find some solace.

Pulling into the parking lot above Lover's Leap, she left the car and battled the wind as she struggled along the beaten path through the wet grass. *Why didn't I bring a hot drink?*

Nearing the spot where she and Derrick had shared countless romantic picnics, Jennie came to a sudden halt, captivated by the seaside rope swing tossing and twirling in the gale-force winds. It veered left then sharply to the right, teasing the wind to catch up. As if embracing the chaos of its surroundings, it danced recklessly, embracing its new-found freedom.

With each gust, the swing soared into the air like a bird in flight, its fibres straining against the force, releasing a melody of creaks and groans. The once slack rope, now taut and quivering with energy, seemed poised to release the wooden seat into the sky.

Jennie was mesmerized by the relentless dance as the swing soared higher and higher, engaging in an aerial ballet that embraced the chaotic wind.

The swing's trajectory seems unpredictable, as though it has a mind of its own, reflected Jennie. She watched in awe as it reached new heights, hanging precariously for a few seconds before succumbing to gravity's pull, hurtling back toward the earth with a rush of air and a euphoric whoosh.

To Jennie, the tumultuous dance of the swing symbolized liberation and resilience. At that moment, she yearned to be free. She knew she was characteristically resilient, but today was different. Yet, as she gazed at the swing's wild dance, a spark ignited within her. What if she resurrected her spirit of adventure, fearlessly surrendering to the wind's whims, and embracing the untamed energy that surrounds it? The spectacle of freedom, grace, and unyielding spirit captivated Jennie, beckoning her to join in its spirited ballet.

Pulling her raincoat tight to close the gap between the top of the zipper and the bare skin of her neck, Jennie tried to stay warm. Kicking clumps of grass away, she searched for somewhere to sit. At first, she perched on top of a rock, with no protection from the wind. She soon chose a more comfortable spot sitting on the sand with her back resting against a big log.

Storm-watching was common on the islands, an event many turned into a reason to party. Today, Jennie didn't feel like celebrating. The sound of the crashing surf mirrored her turbulent soul. As darkness fell, the only light was the wide swath of moonlight cutting across the angry sea. Shivering, Jen longed for someone to hold her tight against the storm.

Instead of feeling comforted by the once-familiar surroundings, Jennie felt nothing but alone in her deepest despair. She felt like a stranger in the place she once felt safe and loved. While visions of Derrick often appeared during her darkest moments, tonight there were none. Instead of the warmth of his embrace, she was surrounded by a cavernous echo, a barren emptiness that denied her the comfort she'd hoped to find.

Jennie hoped she could count on that familiar spiritual connection that had seemed to reinforce her journey after her husband's untimely death. All she felt tonight was abandoned. Abandoned by Derrick's spirit. Abandoned in this physical world by Clay.

Clay didn't abandon you, you pushed him away.

Too cold to stay out any longer, Jennie retraced her steps to the car, using her cell phone flashlight to help her see the path. She had not intended to stay away for so long. Yet, she somehow found a small degree of comfort having revisited a place once sacred to her and Clay. It felt like she was reclaiming a part of him and the closeness they once shared.

The wind had finally died down, and a light rain began to fall.

Once back in her warm house, Jennie removed her dripping raincoat and crept up the stairs trying not to wake Kathleen.

Settling into bed, Jennie fought against any more thinking, but that was impossible. She wasn't one to let things happen *to* her. She refused to be a victim, even though it felt that way sometimes.

Recognizing that she had pushed Clay away, she didn't ask herself, *Can I get him back?*, she asked herself *How can I get him back?*

She had distanced herself from analyzing what she sometimes construed as messages from the spiritual world. But tonight, her mind was restless. She thought hard about what had happened at Lover's Leap, and what she was trying to accomplish by returning there. And then it hit her:

You can't change what happened, but that doesn't mean you have to settle for it.

CHAPTER 24

After completing her chores the next day, Jennie immersed herself in reflective thought. She wandered to the old launch site where Clay had shared his passion for paragliding. The quiet ocean and clear sky accentuated his absence. Remembering his goals of helping students conquer their fear of heights, discouraging risky behaviour, and sharing the joy of flight, Jennie longed for his charismatic presence.

She longed to run her fingers through his messy-curly hair and to feel the thrill of his muscular body against hers.

The melodic ringtone of her phone interrupted her deep thoughts. With all her heart, she hoped it would be Clay.

"Bev, it's so great to hear your voice." Jennie sincerely meant her words; she always had time for Bev. She hadn't spoken with her dear friend for three months now and hadn't heard the details of the girls' trip to Europe in June.

"We missed you, Jen," Bev kindly expressed, but Jennie secretly doubted they'd given her a second thought once they started enjoying the wonders of Europe. Besides, she hadn't exactly kept up her friendships with any of them. Not the way she used to.

"Bev, I'd love to hear all about it." Jennie paused briefly before extending an invitation. "Can you come to the house tonight? We have a lot of catching up to do."

Bev sounded pleased with the invitation, and they agreed to keep it casual. "I'll be there at six," she said and, true to her word, Bev's old VW came rattling up the driveway just as Jennie arrived on the veranda with two glasses of white wine and a charcuterie board.

Jennie hardly had a moment to spare, but she'd made a commitment to herself to open her heart to love, and that involved her friends and family, too. And she was learning to ask for help when she needed it.

Bev and Jennie tried their best to catch each other up on everything that had transpired since their last conversation in mid-March. Eager to reconnect, they made plans to attend the next round of yoga classes together. As Jennie shared the news of her recent breakup with Clay, Bev's expression fell, and her shoulders sagged.

Bev knew all too well that Jennie had lost herself in grieving for Derrick at the expense of living her life to the fullest. Like the loyal friend that she was, Bev quickly offered to do everything she could to help find Clay.

"Is there any possibility he could have returned to Ireland with his ex?" Bev had a concerned expression on her face as if she'd smelled something foul.

The thought sent a shiver down Jennie's spine. Right now, she was determined to follow him anywhere, even if his ex was involved. After all, his written words had suggested an enduring love, and she clung to that sentiment. "You know, he never mentioned a love of Ireland. And I can't see him disconnecting from the life he established here over many years," remarked Jennie, her voice tinged with uncertainty.

"Have you gone to his house? Maybe someone's house-sitting," Bev suggested, and then an idea sparked in her mind. "Hey," she shouted excitedly, "why not call the paragliding association, whatever it's called, or the number in his ad for lessons? Someone must know where he is."

Jennie was pretty sure that his personal cell phone number was the same as the number in his ad, but she would check. "Good ideas, Bev, thanks. If you don't mind, I'll do that right now."

Jennie found Clay's promotional material on her phone and confirmed that the phone numbers were the same. She found the number of the local paraglider's association and listened to a pre-recorded message. Pressing number one to speak with Clay Brookfield, her stomach fluttered with nervous tension when she heard his recorded voice.

Following instructions, she left her name and number, forcing herself to speak calmly in her lower register. He already had her personal information, of course, but she wanted to make an urgent request that he return her call.

Closing the call, Jennie turned to Bev and confessed, "I'm trying not to sound too desperate, but I dearly need to hear from him."

Bev sighed. "Maybe you'll have to board that plane to Ireland after all, Jen." Bev was only half joking. She knew her friend well.

The deep furrow on Jennie's forehead didn't match her perky response. "It is what it is, my friend. Now, how can I find where the former Barbara Brookfield lives in Ireland? If she took his name in marriage, that is."

～

Jennie was up and dressed before the alarm rang at six a.m. the next morning. She made a list of all the people she could call to ask if they knew where Clay went. She even reached out to Ben, the local RCMP officer, who inquired, "Do you wish to file a Missing Persons Report?"

"Uh, well, not exactly, Ben. I mean, I miss him, that's for sure," Jennie began, feeling her words falter. She mentally chided herself for the awkwardness. Stumbling through an explanation, she mentioned the farewell letter but didn't go into detail about something so personal.

Ben clarified it was unnecessary to file a report, but he promised to inform Jennie if he spotted Clay anywhere on the island. He added these words to help comfort his friend: "I don't know where Clay Brookfield is, Jen, but I'm on it. If he's anywhere on the island, I'll find him."

Jennie found solace in knowing she had allies. Even though her custom was to do everything herself, she knew she needed help this time. The way Kathleen had explained it to Jennie years ago made it sound selfish to deny a friend's offer. "It makes people feel good to help, so you do them a favour when you accept."

Eager to complete the day's chores and focus on finding Clay, Jennie descended the stairs to the inviting aroma of freshly brewed coffee in the kitchen.

"Mom, you're a dear. I can't tell you how much I need that coffee this morning."

"It's a good one, too. Funny how even the slightest change in the number of coffee grounds can significantly change the flavour in the cup," Kathleen remarked confidently.

"Well, today I hope the measuring spoon was heaping with

grounds," Jennie replied, filling her coffee mug to the brim and taking a seat at the kitchen table.

"And why, may I ask, do you require an extra injection of caffeine this morning, Jen?" Kathleen asked, good-naturedly. "Does it have anything to do with that envelope Clay dropped off the day before yesterday?"

Jennie choked on her coffee, splattering brown liquid on her T-shirt. Hastily pushing back her chair, she headed to the sink to tear off a paper towel and dry herself. She poured a glass of water and then gulped the entire glass.

"Mom, you mean Clay came to the house?"

Kathleen looked puzzled. "Yes, dear. How else would he drop off the envelope?"

"Where was I when Clay came to the house?" Jennie asked, but before Kathleen could answer, she said, "Oh, right. That was the day I went to the village before the changeovers to help organize the donation centre."

"Yes, I think that's right," Kathleen acknowledged. "He came to say goodbye to me, he said. He seemed to know you weren't home, which I thought was rather odd. And he said he'd written you a letter—I mean, he said it was a letter. I wasn't snooping."

While Jennie normally found Kathleen's coy demeanour endearing, this morning she harboured a burning question.

"Did Clay say where he was going?"

As hard as Jennie tried to hide it, Kathleen could not have missed the intensity in her gaze and the urgency in her voice. Kathleen shifted her position, standing back a little to give herself time to think. She likely didn't want to get this wrong.

"Uh, yes, he mentioned something. Let me think for a minute, dear," she said, looking at the floor. "It was a few days ago."

Jennie had been concerned about her mother's memory

loss. She seemed to recall events in the distant past more rapidly than events in the recent past.

"Here, Mom, please have a seat," Jennie said, pulling out a chair for Kathleen. "I didn't mean to cause you undue concern. Have you had breakfast yet?"

"I have, or at least I think I have." She paused, then added, "When you eat the same thing every morning and follow the same routine, sometimes you forget what day it is," she chuckled.

"Let me boil an egg for you. I'll toast some bread if you'd like that, Mom."

"Oh, no, dear. I'm not hungry. I'll just sip away at my glass of milk," she smiled. "Please don't worry."

Jennie tried to remain calm and not rush her mother. She walked to the kitchen door and looked out into the garden. "This summer's roses are something, aren't they, Mom?"

"Oh, the best I've seen in years, Jen. My favourite is that red-and-white one, called The Fourth of July. That's easy to remember." Kathleen took a sip of milk.

"Yes, just gorgeous. By the way, Mom," Jennie said casually, once again joining Kathleen at the table. "I need to talk to Clay about something, and I wonder if you can let me know where he might be."

Kathleen beamed. "Yes, dear, he said he was going camping for a few days. Somewhere near Tofino. Funny thing is, I thought he said 'glamping'." I didn't have my hearing aids turned up enough, I guess."

CHAPTER 25

*J*ennie found two glamping businesses online and promptly informed Bev before the first breakfast sitting. Meanwhile, Bev arranged to travel by water taxi from Tofino to the glamping sites at Hot Springs Cove the following day. Making a reservation on the ferry from Vesuvius wasn't possible, so they'd have to catch the early-morning run to connect with the small boat charter and arrive at the glamping site before dark.

As she scrolled through online pictures showcasing interiors that resembled hotel rooms more than tents, Jennie couldn't help but wonder what occasion Clay and his female companion were celebrating. Glamorous tenting is not exactly Clay's style, Jennie smirked to herself.

BEV AND JENNIE sat on the veranda in the afternoon. "You know," said Jennie, "maybe I'm wrong about the Find My

Phone app. Perhaps we did share locations. I seem to recall that Clay thought it was a good idea despite any drawbacks."

Bev's eyes widened as she watched Jennie search for the app on her phone. If she had the app and it showed where Clay's devices were, that would eliminate one of the two glamping sites.

"Oh my gosh, that's amazing," Jennie said. "How stupid of me not to check before now. Look at this, Bev." She turned her phone so that Bev could see the map signalling exactly where Clay's phone was in the present moment.

"Oh, and hey," said Bev, "it shows that your cell phone is with you right now." They both laughed at what was obvious to them.

After exchanging ideas, Jennie and Bev agreed—they would not give the glamping site caretakers advance notice of their arrival. They wanted to avoid any possibility of rejection.

Instead, they would show up unannounced, and Jennie would explain to the caretakers that she had an urgent message for Clay Brookfield. The kindest thing, she would say, would be to deliver the message in person.

Surely, faced with heart-breaking news, they reasoned, the caretakers wouldn't refuse such a simple request for kindness.

In the light of day, Jennie couldn't shake the nagging question: Was their plan feasible or just a crazy idea born out of desperation? She understood all too well that desperation seldom led to favourable outcomes—it was never a good starting point or ending point.

While Jennie tackled her daily chores at the B&B, Bev meticulously chartered their route to the glamping site. Their journey would involve two water crossings and a road trip, mirroring Clay and Jennie's trip to Tofino three weeks ago. The difference was the one-hour ride north by water taxi to the glamping site at Hot Springs Cove.

As the day progressed, Jennie grew increasingly hopeful about their strategy. Bidding farewell to Bev until the next morning, Jennie remarked optimistically, "Maybe this plan isn't as outlandish as it first appeared. It seems rather straight-forward."

Buoyed by her team of supporters, including Alexa and Kyla filling in for her at Cliffhouse, Jennie's spirits lifted, fostering a flicker of hope that their collective efforts might yield success.

ONCE THEY ARRIVED in Tofino the next day, they parked the car and eagerly awaited the water taxi. That part of their journey would land them on a rocky coast where they hoped to locate a luxurious tent and a celebratory couple who didn't mind being pried apart for just a few minutes. Jennie tried hard to squelch the slightest negativity that dared to creep into her thoughts.

The water taxi arrived promptly at six p.m., bouncing over turbulent waves. Jennie attempted to suppress the nervousness building within her as they boarded the small vessel and set out toward Hot Springs Cove.

Bev must have sensed her friend's uneasiness as she reached out to squeeze Jennie's forearm.

Jennie managed a smile in acknowledgment, but her eyes revealed a different story than her lips. Oblivious to the beautiful seascape, Jennie couldn't shake an unsettling intuition about what was about to happen, even though the details were unknown. The rhythm of the waves, with their sudden rises and falls, seemed to echo her internal turmoil.

As the water taxi pulled up to the dock, a portion of the glamping site came into view, grounding their mission to the present moment.

Instead of feeling heightened anxiety, a welcome sense of steadiness and purpose unexpectedly infused Jennie. Yet, she remained keenly aware that no amount of mental preparation could fully prepare her for the unknown reality that awaited.

Would we simply approach the tent and call out Clay's name? What if someone else met us instead, such as his female companion?

No, she reprimanded herself, *I refuse to dwell on possibilities that may never occur. I'll just have to trust my instincts and improvise.*

Jennie's strength lay in her determination. She understood that this might be her only opportunity to reconcile with Clay.

Stepping off the water taxi with the assistance of the crew, Jennie and Bev awkwardly navigated the shifting wooden dock.

Chuckling at their clumsiness, they carefully made their way across the dock, balancing themselves as they moved onto the stone pathway leading up to the glamping site.

Once on solid ground, Jennie drew in a deep breath, relishing the invigorating freshness of the surrounding wilderness. She visualized Clay in his jeans and a blue T-shirt with the paragliding logo emblazoned across the front.

Memories flooded her imagination—she vividly recalled running her fingers through his soft, curly hair, and the sensation of his sturdy chest pressed against hers as they shared tender moments.

As an athletic-looking young man wearing a white shirt and blue jeans approached them, Jennie greeted him with a blend of warmth and seriousness, just as she and Bev had practised. Jennie glanced at Bev, who mirrored her demeanour exactly.

"Oh, hello," Jennie ventured, bracing herself for the deception. "I apologize for the intrusion, but I have an urgent message for one of your guests, Clay Brookfield."

The man folded his arms across his chest and seemed to study the woman for a moment before speaking. Reaching out to shake their hands, he introduced himself as Brett.

"And you are?"

"My name is Jennie Mitchell," responded Jennie, her voice steady despite the nerves, "and this is my friend Bev."

"And how are you related to Clay, exactly?"

Jennie swallowed hard, summoning all her courage. "I'm a friend of the family," she stated firmly, meeting Brett's gaze with unwavering determination. "And I have urgent news that I need to deliver in person."

"I see," replied Brett, glancing sideways and repositioning himself on the path. "Urgent news, huh? That sounds worrisome."

But Jennie didn't take the bait. She wasn't about to fabricate more falsehoods to construct a narrative aimed at gaining access to Clay. And she didn't want to weave a web so intricate she'd never see her way out. She held her ground, refusing to engage in further deception.

"I'm sorry to tell you that Clay and his wife, well, I assume she was his wife or girlfriend, or something, checked out yesterday."

Jennie's entire being seemed to deflate in an instant. She felt Bev's light touch behind her left shoulder, a silent reassurance in the face of disappointment. Then, a spark of hope flickered within her as she remembered the Find My Phone app.

"Wait, that can't be right," she implored, her voice tinged with urgency.

"What do you mean?" asked Brett, his brow furrowing in confusion. "I checked them out myself."

Jennie frantically searched her phone until she found the app showing the location of Clay's phone... still at the glamping site.

With a mixture of relief and determination, Jennie thrust her arm forward, showing Brett the depiction on her phone. Bev raised her eyebrows.

Brett's expressionless face told Jennie that her information changed nothing. "Clay left his phone behind, unfortunately. Happens all the time. You wouldn't believe the things people forget while on vacation."

Jennie sensed Brett was about to list the many items people leave behind. She interjected. "Look, I can deliver his phone to him. I'll be seeing him on Monday when he's back home again." Another lie.

"I appreciate that, Jennie, but you can probably understand that I can't release his phone to a stranger." Jennie felt the sting of an arrow probably not intended to hurt.

"No, of course not," she replied, nodding in agreement, even as her mind raced to find a solution to this new predicament. "I'll just call right now, and see if he'd like me to bring his phone with me." Bev opened her mouth as if to speak, but remained silent.

Jennie listened as the phone rang through to Clay's voicemail. Instead of leaving yet another message that would probably get no response from Clay, she hung up. Besides, she wasn't entirely sure she wanted to reveal her whereabouts to Clay just yet. No, her message was too crucial to be left on a voicemail. She wanted to deliver it in person.

"Ah, Clay's not answering. Of course, he doesn't have his cell with him. What was I thinking?" She smiled weakly at Brett and thanked him for his trouble.

With heavy hearts, she and Bev retraced their steps down the stone pathway toward the dock, their shoulders slouched and spirits defeated.

Feeling exhausted by now, Jennie sat on the wet dock, still warm from the afternoon sun. She didn't care anymore about getting her capris wet, and she assumed Bev wouldn't either.

"Have a seat, Bev," she said with a faint smile." Removing her socks and shoes and dangling her bare feet in the cool water, she looked up at Bev's worried face and said, "Thanks for waiting. I really appreciate it. Now, please sit beside me while we mull where to go from here."

Ribbons of orange and pink streaked across the sky as the sun set and reflected in the water before them. They were grateful for their warm jackets against the cool evening air, and the wind had picked up again. Bev and Jennie sat in silence, watching nature's spectacle unfold.

As Jennie revisited her conversation with Brett, she wished it had unfolded differently. She didn't want to discourage Bev, who had invested fully in their mission. Yet deep inside, Jennie felt completely defeated.

"Things worth doing are never that easy, Jen. We both know that," Bev said, offering a comforting pat on Jennie's hand.

"Perhaps we were a tad overconfident but, I mean, you have to be positive if your plan has any chance of working. And it might have worked," she said, "had Clay been where the locator said he would be."

"I blame technology for this fiasco," joked Jennie, hoping to lighten the mood.

Turning to her friend, Bev tried to sound encouraging. "Look at it this way, Jen. You've learned a lot over the past few days. I mean, your decisions now could be life-changing in the future. It's not over yet."

"Thanks, Bev. You're right. I think I'm just too tired to figure out Plan B. Tomorrow is another day."

"I guess we better figure out how on earth we're going to

get home," Bev suggested. "Can we charter another boat back to Tofino, do you know?"

"If not, I guess we'll have to go glamping ourselves. You know—stay in the same tent as Clay and his new love. Wouldn't that be charming?"

Sarcasm wasn't Jennie's usual response, but she was talented at finding humour in certain predicaments.

"I'll go find Brett and see what our options are, if we have any options," Bev offered. She headed up the pathway, leaving Jennie to sit alone on the dock as the sunset met the horizon.

Walking up the path a second time probably seemed to Bev like climbing a tall mountain. But the significance of this journey paled compared to the significance of the first.

Meeting Bev halfway up the path, Brett greeted her with an inquisitive look. "Are you still here?" he asked, his tone tinged with surprise.

"Ah, yes, I'm afraid so. Is there any chance we can get a boat ride back to the mainland?"

"At this time of night, and in July? No, sorry, there'd be nothing available without pre-booking."

"I didn't think so," Bev replied with a hint of resignation. While it wasn't her nature to be sarcastic, perhaps her fatigue got the better of her. "Do you have any suggestions other than Jen and I sleeping out in the open, exposed to the dangers of wildlife and such?"

Brett's expression softened slightly. "You know, if you don't mind spending a few bucks—because glamping isn't cheap-—I have one tent vacant for this evening, because of a cancellation. That's almost unheard of in the summer, and it'd be safer than sleeping out in the open."

Bev paid the fee for the night for both her and Jennie after peeking inside the tent.

⌒

As Jennie sat alone on the dock, exhaustion took over, and her mind wandered into the realm of what-ifs and alternate realities so deeply that she later struggled to recognize what was real and what was not.

In her imagination, she replayed her conversation with Brett, envisioning a different outcome. She imagined a scenario where her urgent message was received with understanding and empathy, and where it was acted upon as she and Bev had hoped.

In her daydream, Brett informed her, "You're in luck because they just finished dinner, and I was about to clear the dishes, so they went to the hot springs to enjoy their wine." Jennie imagined steeling herself for the surprise visit by the hot springs, wondering how she would feel if she were in Clay's shoes.

"Just wait here for a moment, please," she imagined Brett saying, "and I'll let Clay know you're here."

"Yes, thank you, Brett. Please inform him that this is a private matter of some urgency and that I need to speak with him alone," Jennie envisioned herself saying, with composure and empathy.

"All right, I will. I'll let him know," Brett replied.

Jennie pictured Brett walking up over a rocky incline with purpose while she advanced to a platform of flattened rock, waiting to make her next move.

She pictured Bev gently encouraging Jennie with a reassuring, "You've got this," before turning toward the dock and retracing her steps down the path, following their prearranged plan to provide privacy if Clay agreed to meet with Jennie.

Jennie envisioned herself breathless, her heart pounding as

she awaited what was to come. Brett emerged briefly and called over the rocks, "He'll be with you shortly, Jennie."

Standing alone on the rocky platform, anticipating Clay's emergence from the hot springs, Jennie tried to fortify herself, ignoring the weakness in her knees. And just like that, Clay stood up on the rocky hill, bear-chested and with a white towel wrapped around his waist, looking like The Lion King of Hot Springs Cove.

Internally, Jennie gasped, careful not to betray her excitement. She didn't want to appear like a young girl in love for the first time. Yet she was aware this was uncharted territory.

Who, in their right mind, would stalk someone on their vacation, fabricate a lie to get to see him, and then attempt to convince him she wanted him back—while his new companion sipped a glass of wine, waiting for him to rejoin her in the hot springs pool?

Continuing in her daydream, Jennie's heart warmed as she heard Clay's deep voice. "Jen," he exclaimed cheerfully as he approached.

Leaning in for a quick kiss on her lips, he skillfully avoided getting his wet body too close to hers in case she got wet. Jen had an overwhelming desire to wrap herself around Clay and never let him go.

She imagined his curiosity and surprise. "What is this about? What can be so urgent that you travelled all the way here to tell me?" He waited with a slight frown, but a sparkle in his turquoise eyes revealed his delight at seeing her again.

"Clay, I'm so sorry to interrupt your vacation. Don't worry, it's not bad news. I just didn't know any other way to get to see you, especially under the circumstances."

"What circumstances, love? You mean my sudden departure with only a letter to explain?"

In Jennie's imagination, Clay bowed his head. "I'm sorry about that, Jen. That wasn't exactly kind of me, and it's no excuse, but I was quite distraught and felt rather hopeless about our relationship. Please forgive me."

Placing his sensuous lips on the back of her hand, Clay lingered there.

Jennie's stomach thrilled, even though the scenes were all in her head.

Feeling no longer foolish, Jen's confidence soared with Clay's gentle touch and heartfelt words. "Baby, I've missed you so much, you can't even imagine. And I'm here to ask for your forgiveness and understanding. I want you back."

Jennie had called no one 'baby' in a long time. The tenderness she felt at using that word made her heart sing even though she was only daydreaming.

The softness of Clay's eyes showed Jennie that he held no hard feelings against her for the way their relationship had played out.

"Jen, I love what you're saying. I do." Clay beckoned her to sit with him on a driftwood log by the side of the path. "But how have things changed, honey?"

Jennie was prepared for this. "I finally realize that you are my new forever man, or at least I hope you are."

She wrapped her right arm across his shoulders and touched the back of his neck, sweeping her hand up through his damp curls.

But she wanted to explain. "You know, you were right, Clay, when you said that I could never move forward if I kept hanging on to Derrick. I don't know why it took me so long to understand that."

Clay wrapped his left arm around Jennie and pulled her close. "Oops, sorry, babe. I didn't want to wet your clothes."

Jennie stood up and sat on Clay's lap, facing him, with her legs wrapped around his body. "Go ahead, get me wet, baby."

She placed her lips on his and they embraced with such

passion Jennie could feel both their hearts pounding in their chests. When they finally released each other, Jennie said, "I want to share my dream with you, Clay, when we can have long conversations without interruptions, maybe in our favourite spot at Lover's Leap. Would that be all right with you, hon?"

"More than all right, babe. I'll be back home on Monday after I see my sister off."

"Your sister? Oh, I forgot you had a sister living on the mainland. Did she visit you recently on Sunrise Island?"

"Yes, for a couple of nights. And then I booked this glamping experience for her. I knew she'd love it."

A big smile appeared on Clay's tanned face. "C'mon up. I'd like to introduce you."

~

... But that was only fiction, and when Bev startled Jennie back into reality by shouting to her from the gravel path, she felt disoriented.

So deeply invested was Jennie in her daydream, that it took her some time to realize that none of this had happened.

"A new adventure," Bev proclaimed, happy they had secured a safe place to spend the night.

"Yes," replied Jennie with a smile that seemed almost to herself. "That's what I'm all about from here on in," she continued. "Life's too short."

"I'll drink to that—if there's anything left to drink in this luxury wilderness place," said Bev, hopeful they weren't too late for dinner.

~

BRETT DIRECTED them to glamorous tent Number One, the tent closest to the shoreline. The glamping business typically arranged the tents with enough distance between them to ensure privacy for everyone. Jennie couldn't conceal her astonishment.

"Now this is my idea of camping," she joked, eyeing the lavish canopy bed draped in flowing gossamer fabrics. "This looks like a high-end hotel suite."

A resplendent crystal chandelier hung gracefully from a gleaming polished wooden beam. Sleek black marble elephants formed the base of two bedside lamps, while soft, ambient light emanated from within their silk shades, casting a warm, romantic glow inside the tent. Persian rugs and a plush upholstered sofa and chair added to the ambiance of comfort and opulence.

Stepping to the private outside lounge area, Jennie and Bev settled into a pair of bamboo chairs with sumptuous turquoise cushions designed with a peacock motif. They relaxed, enveloped by the rhythmic sound of the surf crashing against the rocks below.

Immersed in the serenity of their surroundings, Jennie savoured the peacefulness of the forest at night.

In the distance, they heard a slapping sound out on the water. As the sound grew louder, they realized it was a boat bouncing over the waves.

"Pirates?" asked Bev, a hint of playful suspense lingering in her voice.

"Quick, hide the treasures," quipped Jennie. "More importantly, let's get Brett to pop open that bottle of bubbly I spotted in the ice bucket."

With a mischievous grin, she rose from her chair and went in search of the elusive Brett. *I thought he'd be more attentive, considering the price.*

Outside the tent, a sparkling tapestry of stars adorned the night sky. Jennie could hear a couple of male voices in the distance. She moved closer toward the dock, wondering if Brett was talking with someone.

It was too dark for her to see the faces of the figures, but she stopped short when she thought she recognized Clay's voice. She couldn't resist the urge to investigate further.

Walking slowly down the path toward the dock, Jennie got close enough to hear what they were saying.

"Did you catch her name?" asked Clay.

"Jennie something. In fact," said Brett, "she's still here. And she offered to take your phone home and deliver it to you, but you know I couldn't release it without your permission."

Silence. Clay looked upward as Jennie descended the pathway toward the dock.

"Oh, here she is now, Clay. I'll leave you two alone..." Before he could leave, Jennie said to him, "Brett, would you kindly pour a glass of bubbly for my friend Bev? She's waiting for me in the lounge."

"Yes, of course. I'll do that right now and I'll bring you an assortment of hors d'oeuvres before dinner."

"Thank you. She'll love that."

Clay disembarked from the gently rocking boat, finding his footing on the dock while Brett headed in the opposite direction. Clay reached out to help Jennie onto the dock, apparently neither of them considering standing on solid ground.

As they stood facing each other, silence enveloped them until Jennie reached out and gently touched Clay's shoulder, uncertain of his response.

"Clay, I can't tell you how happy I am to see you. You can't fathom how many imaginary conversations I've had with you since I read your letter," Jennie confessed.

"Oh, the letter," Clay murmured, glancing out to sea for a

moment before continuing. "That's not something I'm proud of, Jen. Do you want to talk about it?" he offered thoughtfully.

"I want to talk about that and a lot more," Jennie said. "But there's one thing I want you to know right now."

"What's that, baby?" Clay's voice was tender, and he lightly placed both hands on Jennie's waist.

Jennie spoke with a quiet certainty. "I love you, Clay, and I want you to know that I'm ready to delve into the next layer of our relationship, wherever it may lead. As long as it's with you, I'm all in," she emphasized.

Jennie wrapped her arms around Clay's shoulders and pressed her lips against his. He drew her in close and they kissed under the stars until the dock quivered beneath them, challenged by more forceful waves that playfully teased their dry shoes and altered their sense of balance.

But Jennie held strong like the rope of the swing, ready to soar with abandon.

WALKING HAND-IN-HAND UP THE PATHWAY, Clay asked, "Are you and Bev staying the night?"

"Let's put it this way, babe. My best friend on earth is sitting in a glamorous tent sipping on sparkling wine, maybe even champagne, I don't know. She deserves to enjoy all the luxury in the world because she's the epitome of the world's best friend. She's the real deal," Jennie proclaimed.

"And, as much as I'd love to spend the night with my true love, I'm going to stick with our plans," Jennie confirmed.

"I understand," said Clay. "Loyal friends are hard to find. It's just that if she wanted to, and only if she wanted to, she could return to Tofino in the boat. The captain is waiting for me to return after claiming my phone."

"And that's exactly what I want to do, people," Bev shouted from the outdoor lounge, a glass of bubbly in her hand. "I wouldn't dream of getting in between your joyous reunion. After all, this is the outcome we were all hoping for."

"Oh, Bev, I wouldn't dream of it," protested Jennie.

"No, no, this is my call," Bev shouted back. "Clay, would you mind speaking with the captain, please? I'm ready to go now."

Clay turned to Jennie. "Is it okay? It seems like the lady has spoken, yes?"

"Bev, you're the best." Jennie placed her right hand over her heart as she said those words, and Bev was quick to respond.

"I know, I know. I overheard what you said about me, so you're good for at least another decade."

Both Jennie and Clay saw Bev off after arranging accommodation for her in Tofino. She'd drive Jennie's car to Nanaimo and retrace the route they took that same day.

"I love you," Jennie shouted over the motor as the boat pulled away. The new Jennie strived to love bigger, wider, and more often. This was a good start.

"HEY, handsome, want to sit in the hot springs pool with me on this starry, starry night?" Jennie's voice dripped with playful allure as she beckoned Clay.

"I'm there, Sweet Lady. I'll get Brett to bring some champagne and towels. Did you bring a bathing suit?" Clay asked with a glint in his eye that Jen could see even in the evening light.

"You know I didn't. And I know that it just doesn't matter," Jennie replied, with a hint of mischief in her voice.

"Right," agreed Clay. Two wild people in the wilderness on a Saturday night."

"Oh, I love this," exclaimed Jennie as she settled into the warm water and took her first sip of chilled champagne. "But I love you even more."

The sense of freedom and rightness of finally expressing those words filled Jennie with immense satisfaction.

A relaxed calm enveloped Jennie so that she eventually felt comfortable enough to ask Clay a burning question: "Okay, Clay, I have to ask—who was that woman—the woman you spent the night with here, last night, I guess it was."

"Oh, ha! Yes, I guessed that might concern you, Jen; I'm surprised you didn't ask earlier," Clay replied with a playful grin, avoiding the question.

Lifting his champagne glass and clinking Jennie's in a light-hearted toast, Clay changed the subject.

"Just look at that night sky, Jen. It's like a canvas painted just for us, don't you think?"

"Clay," she said, shaking her head with a smile.

"Alright, alright," he chuckled. "You're talking about the young redhead in the sunglasses and capris, right?"

"Enough with the jokes," Jennie said, leaning in closer to him.

"That was Olivia, my little sister, of course," Clay said reassuringly. "Who else would it be?"

CHAPTER 26

Sunrise lit up the east side of the tent, welcoming Jennie and Clay to Saturday morning. The luxurious bed beckoned them to linger, so they languished there for hours, revelling in their shared passion.

As Jennie and Clay leisurely enjoyed a late breakfast in the outside lounge overlooking the ocean, a pod of orcas appeared, as if orchestrated at just the right moment.

A mesmerizing sight unfolded as their dorsal fins pierced the surface, rising and falling in synchronized movements. Their acrobatic leaps sent them soaring, momentarily defying gravity before they gracefully dove back beneath the sea. In this enchanting display of grace and power, the orcas called to each other in a language known only to them.

"That's how I see our connection, Clay—harmonious and wild," Jennie remarked, smiling with delight as she picked up a luscious-looking strawberry, clasping it between her teeth, leaving just enough for Clay to savour.

Leaning in to take his bite, Clay's delight mirrored that of a boy with a candy bar.

As he dabbed the vibrant red strawberry juice from his lips onto the crisp white linen napkin, he marvelled at the sentiment. "Oh, you have changed, my darling Jen. I fell in love with you the way you were. But this..."

Clay raised his champagne flute filled with mimosa and air-toasted the new Jen.

CHAPTER 27

*J*ennie and Clay didn't spend much time together for the next two weeks, although they exchanged texts every day. They would exchange waves when they caught sight of each other in the mornings, Clay on his way to the launch site, and Jennie on her way to do the changeovers.

One morning, she spotted him on a tandem flight, something he rarely did, he had told her. Yet Jennie was extra busy these days, with the peak summer season upon her, and she hardly found time to notice much else.

The next morning, as Jennie headed toward the kitchen with a full load of laundry, she noticed Clay setting up his equipment on the launch site. It was particularly windy, and she tightened her grip on the laundry basket just as the wind caught it.

Perfect conditions for paragliding, she mused, imagining Clay's easy launch. When the wind caught his parachute, she smiled, enjoying watching him engage in something he loved.

Reaching for the metal handle of the screen door, Jennie's

thoughts were interrupted by a distant cry. *Or was it just a seagull's call?*

Uncertain of the source, Jennie strained to listen. The next cry sounded like it was coming from the direction of the clifftop.

Her heart quickened as she raced toward the launch site. Peering over the edge, horrified, she spotted the red and yellow parachute emblazoned with Clay's company logo, sprawled over driftwood logs and rocks of various sizes.

What she initially mistook for two narrow logs protruding from beneath the parachute, she soon realized were Clay's blue jean-clad legs and his black boots.

"No," Jennie cried into the wind, her hair swept in every direction, and the fabric of her loose cotton shirt billowing like Clay's parachute below.

Racing back to the kitchen, she dialled 9-1-1 away from the wind, her fingers trembling as she reached the operator.

Not waiting for the usual questions, Jennie blurted, "Ambulance. I need an ambulance right away. There's been a serious paragliding accident right below Cliffhouse by the Sea."

Struggling to keep her composure, Jennie begged, "Please hurry… I don't know if he's even alive."

Grabbing her emergency kit from the front hall, Jennie was solely focused on Clay's wellbeing. She raced to her SUV, aware that she had a warm blanket stowed in the trunk.

Resting her cell phone on the passenger seat, she deftly found the beach access closest to the accident site, her heart pounding with fear and desperation.

Please, please be okay, she pleaded silently, unable to bear the thought of losing another loved one. *Loved one.* The words echoed in her mind, and she bit her lip anxiously.

Hurrying toward Clay with her blanket and emergency kit

in hand, Jennie noticed a stream of blood trickling over the wet sand.

Acting quickly, she peeled away the parachute, fully exposing Clay's injured form.

"I'm here, darling. Can you hear me?" she cried, gently laying the blanket on top of him, hoping it would provide some comfort. Checking for a pulse on his left wrist, she thought she detected a weak beat.

Jennie continued to speak to Clay, forcing herself to remain calm, although she was dying inside. "I'm here, Clay. You're going to be okay... I love you."

As the paramedics hurried to the site, Jennie placed her hand on Clay's forearm, hoping he could sense her presence.

Quickly assessing Clay's condition, the paramedics worked to stabilize him as best they could, immobilizing his legs and supporting his head as they expertly rolled him onto his back. As additional emergency responders arrived, they carefully lifted Clay onto a stretcher and carried him to the waiting ambulance.

Jennie watched anxiously, her heart heavy with concern, and tears welling in her eyes. She followed the entourage closely behind, climbing into the ambulance to provide any information that might be helpful.

While she was seated in a small fold-out chair out of the attendant's way, she fastened her seatbelt as instructed, preventing her from holding Clay's hand. As the ambulance sped off toward the hospital, she said a silent prayer for his recovery.

At Lady Minto, the medical team determined that Clay would be air-lifted to Vancouver General Hospital, due to the extent of his injuries. When asked if she was his next of kin, Jennie told them she was his girlfriend.

All she knew about his former wife was her first name, Barbara, and that she lived somewhere in Dublin. His son Patrick, she said, was still in Dublin as far as she knew. On her phone, she searched for a 'Patrick Brookfield" living in Dublin. Nothing helpful came up.

Jennie would accompany Clay on the airlift to Vancouver General. Kyla took a leave of absence from the vet's office and came to stay with Kathleen and tend to the B&B guests as best she could.

JENNIE SAT among others in the hospital waiting room as Clay was rushed to the emergency room.

Hours later, Jennie struggled to keep her eyes open as the attending medical doctor approached, introducing herself as Dr. Kingsley. Taking a seat beside Jennie, Dr. Kingsley asked, "Were you able to contact Clay's family?"

Jennie's heart sank at the mention of next of kin. "I'm sorry. I couldn't find a Patrick Brookfield in Dublin," she replied, her voice trembling with worry.

Dr. Kingsley gently informed Jennie of Clay's condition, detailing multiple fractures, including two broken legs, as well as a head injury.

"He's in intensive care now, still unconscious, but we're closely monitoring his condition, and doing everything we can for him," she assured.

"It's important that he receives the best care possible at this critical stage," Dr. Kingsley emphasized, pausing to give Jennie a chance to process the information.

"Is he going to survive?" Jennie asked bravely.

"We don't know. We may have more answers over the next 24 hours." Dr. Kingsley responded with a hint of a smile.

"May I stay with Clay in his room?" Jennie inquired, uncertain of the protocol.

"Since you are his sole supporter at the moment, I think it would be a very good idea if you stayed by his side," she advised, understanding the importance of familiar faces during recovery. I'll make sure arrangements are made for you to stay with Clay in his room."

CLAY SPENT two full days in the ICU, slowly opening his eyes on the third day just as Jennie attempted the second verse of "Don't Close Your Eyes," by Keith Whitley. Singing became Jennie's solace, a way to pass the time and ease her anxieties as she kept vigil by Clay's bedside.

Initially disoriented, Clay gradually seemed to regain his bearings as Jennie comforted him, offering reassurance that he would continue to improve with time.

She remained by his side throughout the ordeal as he underwent various procedures, treatments, and tests. As Clay fought to recover, Jennie offered words of encouragement, and love as Clay began his long road to recovery.

CHAPTER 28

The months passed by even more quickly, it seemed to Jennie, filled with care for Clay and cherished moments with Kathleen.

With room in her house to accommodate Clay during his recovery, Jennie didn't hesitate to step up when Dr. Kingsley asked, "Is there someone to attend to his medical needs when I release him from the hospital?"

As summer turned to fall, Jennie's dedication to Clay's well-being and appreciation of his presence in her life were evident to all. The love expressed in Clay's eyes whenever she was in the room was sustaining enough, but when he said, "I love everything about you, Jen. You make me want to open my eyes every day," she felt treasured.

Kathleen, although increasingly frail and struggling with low blood pressure, appeared happy spending her days sitting in her favourite spot on the veranda as the sun filtered through the trees on the eastern side of the house. With her two wishes fulfilled, Kathleen was a picture of contentment and gratitude.

"You know," she commented to Jennie, her beloved

companion for morning coffee visits, along with Rollo, "I think Clay recovered all the faster in your care."

Jennie smiled, acknowledging the validity of her mother's observation. "He's almost fully healed now, although we don't know what long-term effects might loom."

Taking a sip of her rich roasted coffee, Jennie added, "I'm just grateful that he's still here with us." Her eyes still welled with tears whenever she reflected on the accident, which remained vividly etched in her mind.

Jennie rose from the chaise longue and stretched, raising her arms high into the air. "Before I clean up the kitchen, I'm going to take a stroll over to the clifftop. Check it out for Clay," she said brightly.

It was one of those mornings that Jennie couldn't resist. These days, she tended to celebrate moments rather than doggedly tackling one chore after another. She had Clay to thank for that.

Gazing across the Channel, the dance of sunshine on the water captivated Jennie. She reflected on the day she visited Clover Point shortly after Derrick's death. The same day a passerby had shared with her the tale of "The Little Mermaid of Copenhagen".

True to the vow she made that day, she thought of her dearly beloved as she witnessed the sparkle of sunshine on the Salish Sea.

Appreciating the simple pleasures of life, Jennie noticed a patch of spent dandelions by the arbutus tree, and memories of her last day in the garden with Derrick flashed across her mind.

"Yes, and if you can blow all the seeds off with a single

breath, then the person you love will love you back," Jennie had explained in a playful tone, glancing at Derrick and catching his smile.

Seizing the moment, Jennie plucked a spent dandelion and, with a single exhale, sent the entire collection of seeds floating into the air.

The one I love will love me back. Confident she'd found a second true love in Clay, Jennie thanked the universe for the gifts of love that had come her way.

With Clay by her side, Jennie felt empowered to face the challenges ahead and looked forward to what the rest of the year might bring.

As she watched the dandelion seeds gracefully return to the ground, symbolizing new beginnings, she embraced the continuing story of life at Cliffhouse by the Sea, anticipating the adventures that awaited.

THANK you so much for reading *Cliffhouse by the Sea.* I hope you enjoyed the story.

Ready to immerse yourself in the captivating world of the Mitchell family, experiencing the highs and lows of their extraordinary everyday lives on Sunrise Island?

If you'd like to be notified when the next book in the series is released AND receive an EXCLUSIVE free copy of the series prequel, *Cliffhouse Footprints,* please scan the QR code below. <u>You can't get this book anywhere else.</u>

Or sign up on my website for updates, discounts, giveaways, and outtakes from my life.

Here's the prequel description below...

CLIFFHOUSE FOOTPRINTS
Book Description

KATHLEEN MITCHELL LONGS TO be a mother before her biological clock ticks out. After trying for two years, she and John consider adoption. She visualizes a newborn baby nestled in her arms, with skin as soft as the petals of a delicate flower. But when life takes an unexpected turn and Kathleen's eight-year-old nephew comes to live with them during his mother's battle with cancer, their plans are upended.

Amidst the emotional whirlwind of caregiving, Kathleen

discovers profound truths about the essence of parental love—a love that transcends blood ties. From heartbreak to unexpected joys, their journey illuminates the transformative power of love and the resilience of the human spirit.

Cliffhouse Footprints, the Sunrise Island Series prequel, celebrates the undeniable force that drives parents to protect, nurture, and support their children through any circumstances.

Follow Kathleen in her transformative journey in this clean women's fiction prequel, a celebration of those who care for children everywhere.

ABOUT THE AUTHOR

Captivated by the intrigue of everyday life, Maren Hill writes heartfelt, emotional stories that celebrate women and the relationships that define their lives.

A wealth of life experience inspires her contemporary small-town beach reads and family sagas where happy endings await.

Quirky characters you'd love to know and stories laced with romance, humour, compassion, and inspiration are trademarks of Maren Hill books.

If you enjoy my books, please leave a review. There's nothing more motivational than positive reviews.

www.ingramcontent.com/pod-product-compliance
Lightning Source LLC
Chambersburg PA
CBHW051224210726
48290CB00003B/791